T0001825

PENGUIN METRO READS

IT WAS ALWAYS YOU

Sudeep Nagarkar has authored thirteen bestselling novels, including *Few Things Left Unsaid, That's the Way We Met, It Started with a Friend Request, Sorry, You're Not My Type, You're the Password to My Life, You're Trending in My Dreams, She Swiped Right into My Heart, All Rights Reserved For You, Our Story Needs No Filter, She Friend-Zoned My Love, The Secrets We Keep, Stand By Me, A Second Chance* and, his last release, *Happily Never After*.

All his books combined have sold more than a million copies and continue to be on bestseller lists. He has been featured on the *Forbes India* longlist of the most influential celebrities for two consecutive years. He was also awarded the 'Celebrity Author of 2013' title by Amazon. In 2016, he was named the 'Youth Icon of India' by Zee Awards and the 'Best Fiction Novelist of the Year' by WBR Group. He has given guest lectures at various renowned institutes, including IITs, IIMs and NITs, and has spoken at TEDx.

Connect with Sudeep on social media platforms, where he interacts with more than half a million fans.

Facebook fan page: facebook.com/sudeepnagarkar

Facebook profile: facebook.com/nagarkarsudeep

Twitter handle: @sudeep_nagarkar

Instagram: @sudeepnagarkar

Prologue

He realized he still loved her. It had been a while since the relationship had ended and he was happily married now. But memories of those days with her, memories buried deep in his mind, resurfaced after many years.

Yes, you can still feel affection for a person years after the relationship has ended. So what if it didn't work out back then? After all, you saw something good in each other. Every relationship that you form on the way to who you are leaves an indelible mark on your life.

Be that as it may, is it okay to turn your back on your marriage and not give a thought to whether what you're doing is morally right or wrong?

Karan had no answer to this, and therefore, when we met that afternoon, he shared his dilemma with me. I was stunned by his revelation, as I knew Shruti, the girl he had eventually married, and believed she was certainly the right person for him.

'*Bhai*, relationships are not like sitcoms, with a different plot every week. It's the same story with the same person. Are you doubting whether you've married the right girl or not, at this juncture, now, when you're about to become a father?' I demanded, trying to read his mind. We were in the car. The traffic on Godbunder Road near my house was already irritating me, and his revelation really got my goat. I tried to concentrate on the road, but my thoughts were focused on him. He was always texting someone on his phone, and now I was sure he was chatting with the same girl he had just been talking about.

I patiently waited for his response. He eventually turned to me and scowled, 'Did I say that? I can't stop myself. I'm attracted to her. I still care for her—because I'm human, with sensitivities, empathies and weaknesses, which I wish I could overcome; because it's possible to still have feelings for someone even if that person treated you badly in the past; because feelings don't just go away because we want them to. It wasn't intentional. It just happened after we met coincidentally.'

'And have you said anything about this to Shruti?' I asked, shifting gears as I finally saw a clear stretch of road ahead.

'Of course not. You're the only one with whom I've shared this.' His face fell, fully realizing the fix he was in.

They say that old love is like old wine. But, if an old love comes back into your life when you are not only in another relationship but married and about to be a father, that same old wine can give you a terrible hangover for the rest of your life.

I took a deep breath, not quite knowing how to react. For some time, I just kept driving, but Karan noticed the uneasiness on my face and asked, 'Now, why are you quiet? It's not as easy as you thought, right?'

'Look, I understand ... but we're not merely talking about your missing your ex or having a soft corner for her in your heart.' I was trying to make him understand the consequences of the step he wanted to take. 'You actually want her to be in your life ... but that's bullshit!' My voice rose. 'Come on; Shruti loves you so much. And you love her as well; we've all seen the warmth in your relationship. And now, when you're about to enter a new phase, you're making a mess of it. This is the time that she needs you the most. She's pregnant. Have you even thought about what would happen if she came to know about this crap?'

'That's the whole point. It's still not too late, and I don't want any regrets later,' Karan said in a perplexed voice.

The past is emotionally deeper than the future. Tomorrow, we'll still be there. Even if the future is uncertain, it's possible to believe we'll be there. However, we cannot be physically present in the past. It's just a memory. And Karan recollected one such memory with Shruti when he had shared his past relationship with her before getting married. She had said,

'As long as it has nothing to do with your present and future, it's irrelevant. I'm not someone who will judge you just because you were in a relationship. I really appreciate that you chose to tell me, because this by itself tells me how serious you are about this relationship. I don't want to go into the details of your past relationship. All I want you to know is that your past won't ever come in between us.'

Shruti's reaction had all his heart, and Karan wanted to hug her tightly to show her how much her wisdom and understanding meant to him. At the time, he had moved on from his past and had been determined to keep things transparent and open in his marriage. At least, that was what he thought and believed. In fact, he was overjoyed that Shruti had accepted his past as an integral part of him. He loved the maturity and graciousness with which she had understood what he had wanted to convey and why. It was for this very reason that Karan had felt that she was the right girl for him; with time, he realized he had made the right decision by marrying her. Shruti truly loved him and understood his wants and needs. He couldn't have asked for anyone better, but here he was, sitting beside me and debating whether he should go back to a girl who never really cared for him.

When she dumped me, and never saw the misery she caused me, it was abundantly clear that she was selfish and incapable of loving anyone but herself. I reconfigured my life without that person in it and married someone who truly cares for me—loves only me and thinks about me all the time. And now, I should only think about her. This is what my brain says every day. Simple. Logical. But my heart begs to disagree: she does care. She still needs me. She's still struggling without me and needs me to guide her. Deep down, I still love her. Being married to someone doesn't mean I have an off switch for my feelings. Morally, this may not be right, and people may criticize me, but should I really place this sanctimonious society above my feelings? But what about Shruti? What about the new life she is carrying inside her?

Karan was wholly preoccupied as I continued driving. I could gauge his thoughts to an extent. Nevertheless, I couldn't ignore the tornado of panic swirling inside me, regarding Jasmine. Something I hadn't shared with Karan yet, as I felt it wasn't the right time. I had actually wanted to confide in him that evening, which was why I had arranged to meet him; but considering his present quandary, I felt it would be better to keep my problems to myself for the time being.

I touched his shoulder to snap him out of his reverie. 'You know there'll always be a spark left in the heart. You don't need to quench it; nevertheless, it's always better to keep such flames under a fire blanket, otherwise they could burn down your entire house.'

'Now don't go all metaphorical with me. I genuinely want you to help me out in this situation.'

'What the fuck am I supposed to do? It's not a novel in which I frame the incidents according to my wish and will. You're the one who has to make the decision. And I've already told you what I think. Like you said, it's still not too late and, trust me, I too don't want you to have any regrets later.'

'Maybe,' said Karan, 'maybe I will regret it, but will it kill us to try? To put in every bit of effort? I mean, this is our life we're talking about. We don't just walk away when things get difficult, right?'

His words struck me like a bolt of lightning. In the last twenty-four hours, my life had turned upside down when Jasmine had walked out—leaving our house and leaving me. It was my fault, and I was guilty. But she had just walked away without giving me a chance to explain. And here I was, giving relationship advice to my friend, Karan, when my own relationship was badly fucked up. We had been married for three years, and it wasn't like we hadn't had arguments before; but this was beyond serious, and all I could do was bitterly blame myself for it. Only yesterday, I had posted our picture on Instagram and everyone had told us that our relationship was like a fairy tale. But what people tend to forget is that, in real life, relationships require much more than those lovey-dovey pictures that are uploaded on Instagram. Just as every other couple did, we too had our conflicts, but we kept those to ourselves. I wish I could erase that episode and rewrite it as I do in my books—but life doesn't have a backspace button.

I picked up the phone that I had placed on the dashboard, and with one hand still on the steering wheel, I re-dialled Jasmine's number. This was the umpteenth time I was calling her in the past few hours, hoping that she would talk to me at least once and give me a chance to clarify things. Her phone remained unreachable.

I opened our WhatsApp chat and, with my gaze switching between the road ahead and the mobile screen, I texted her, 'Why are you doing this? You know I didn't mean to hurt you. Please call me back.'

I didn't realize I had jumped a red light at the roundabout and a car, which was hurtling towards us from the right, almost rammed into us. I yanked up the emergency brake and our car screeched to a halt. I snapped back to my senses. As I rested my head on the steering wheel, I realized that my negligence could have proved fatal for both Karan and me. Karan had braced himself against the dashboard to avoid slamming into it. His screams to me to stop at the red light had fallen on deaf ears.

'What the fuck are you doing, dude? Are you all right?' he shouted.

Everything wasn't all right. Neither with him, nor with me, and neither of us knew how to untangle the chaos we were trapped in.

Chapter 1

It had been a long day at the office for Karan with a couple of meetings scheduled with clients and last week's performance-analysis meet with his team. It had completely slipped his mind that his father had asked him to come home early because they had arranged to visit a potential bride's family that evening. That morning, over breakfast, when he had told his dad, as he had done several times before, that he wanted to be financially stable before settling down, his father had, as always, unequivocally shot down this plan. To Karan's consternation, unlike their previous sallies to meet with matrimonial alliances, this time around it felt like his parents really meant business; as per the traditional customs, his parents had armed themselves with gifts and boxes of sweets for the girl's family. Karan, stuck in the client meeting, hadn't been reachable when his father had tried contacting him to tell him that his mother was on tenterhooks now because their hosts had called to find out the reason for their delay. Furthermore, it was an hour-long journey.

'I don't understand why these young boys keep mobile phones when they can't answer the calls when needed,' his father grumbled. 'I don't understand how your son can be so careless!' He had already given his word to the family and was now worried that Karan would find a way to slime out of the commitment yet again and he would be left with egg on his face.

'That's great! Whenever he behaves irresponsibly, he is my son and a few months ago, when he got promoted as team manager, he was yours,' Karan's mother responded tartly.

'Do we really want to get into this debate at such a time?'

With an annoyed expression, Karan's mother retreated into the bedroom to text him from her phone and find out what the delay was about.

Karan read the message, concluded the meeting quickly, and rushed to his car to get to the office, which was a few minutes away. He had been working with a tech start-up in Andheri for the last couple of years and had been given the responsibility of bringing funding from companies along with handling clients.

'Papa is going to kill me today if I am late. I guess I should call and convince him to postpone the meeting, if possible,' he thought to himself.

He drove as fast as he could so that he could wrap up the formalities in office and leave quickly. That was when another thought struck him, 'Why am I hurrying so much? If I was late for this meeting, won't the girl's family realize that I'm not interested in this alliance?'

He relaxed and called his mother, 'Mum,' he wheedled, 'can't we postpone the meeting? Even if I came home now, I'm going to be late anyway because I'll have to get ready before we leave. Please, can you convince Papa?'

Karan wasn't aware that his mother had put her mobile on speaker-phone mode and his father had heard him.

He instantly reacted, 'Karan,' he thundered, 'don't make any excuses! I know exactly what you're trying to do here, but I won't budge. I've made a commitment to them. We'll leave for their place now and you can come there directly. It'll save time. I'll WhatsApp the location to you.'

Karan sighed. He knew there was no escape. 'When you have to book a cab or follow Google-Maps instructions, you're helpless; and now you suddenly turn hi-tech when it comes to my marriage.'

'Don't talk nonsense. I know their address, and Shruti's father has sent me their location on WhatsApp. I am just forwarding it. Be there in an hour.'

'Papa, is this really necessary? Didn't we discuss all this in the morning?' Karan protested in a last-ditch attempt to protect his bachelor status.

'Yes, we did; and I told you she's a nice girl. I've known their family for almost a decade now. She'll be compatible with you, and trust me, she'll bring stability to your life. Plus, now is the right time because you're in a good position, with a decent income, to start a family.

In our days, we had other responsibilities apart from handling our own finances. What problems do you have?'

'Oh my God, let's not go into how you did things in your time, please. I'm coming. Just send me the location,' Karan ended the conversation knowing he couldn't win this argument with his old man. He quickly freshened up in the office and left.

Karan wasn't someone who was afraid of relationships. He had dated a girl before and had been fully committed even then. But dating is a different kettle of fish. Marriage entails many more responsibilities, and he wasn't sure if he would be able to manage all of them smoothly. He earned enough to lead a comfortable life, but the pressure of having to handle a family on his own bothered him. Nevertheless, he made up his mind to give it a go; not solely because of parental pressure but by realizing that one day this step would be inevitable. All he wanted and wished for was for the girl to be happy with him and to reciprocate his affection.

* * *

Karan and his parents managed to reach on time, somewhat. They were greeted cordially by Shruti's parents. After they were seated, Shruti's mother disappeared into the inner room to see if her daughter was ready. Karan noticed Shruti's father staring disapprovingly at his attire and realized that he was dressed too casually for the occasion, as opposed to them, clad in proper ethnic wear.

'I'm sorry. I've come directly from office, so . . . didn't really have the time to change.'

'Oh, I understand the work pressure you guys go through,' acceded Shruti's father politely, pretending to accept this lame excuse. They carried on with their casual conversation. A silence fell when Shruti and her mother entered the living room. Although this wasn't the first time, he had seen her, Karan had never before looked at her in the light of a potential partner; he was completely bowled over by her beauty. He had the maturity to realize that there was much more to a relationship than a person's appearance. He wanted to speak to her before making his decision. In any case, that didn't stop him from ogling her while she served the snacks and talked with his parents. She seemed kind and compassionate; Karan drummed his fingers on his thigh nervously as he sneaked glances at her. He hardly knew her, although they had met a few times in the past during family functions and had exchanged nods and greetings. He admired the way her dark eyes crinkled at the corners whenever she smiled.

'Hi, how are you?' Shruti tried to strike up a conversation when she finally decided that Karan was too shy to break the ice. Both sets of parents eyed them curiously, keen to eavesdrop on their conversation.

Karan blurted the first thing that came to his mind, 'I . . . you just . . . you look . . . beautiful.'

Shruti blushed and smiled, dropping her gaze shyly. Appalled at this faux pas, Karan looked around guiltily. But their audience was smiling benignly this time.

Karan scowled. 'What?! Carry on . . . continue your conversation,' Karan said to his parents.

'Of course,' said Shruti's mother, 'we will. But you two should also talk.' This was the cue to her daughter to take him inside so they could converse in private. Karan felt that this was probably the most awkward phase of an arranged marriage's preliminary meeting. This was when you had to second guess the other person's line of thought in order to not come across as a complete idiot.

Karan's heart was beating fast as he followed Shruti to the balcony of her room. Although Shruti had butterflies in her stomach as well, this wasn't her first time, and she was slightly used to the cycle of such meetings and the course of the conversations. Nevertheless, she still was still beset by nerves as always. The only thing that made her slightly comfortable on this particular occasion was that Karan wasn't a total stranger, unlike the long parade of guys she had previously met.

They gazed at the view from the balcony. Karan broke the awkward silence, 'I'm sorry if I embarrassed you. I shouldn't have been so outspoken in front of our parents. I didn't really know what to say.'

Shruti smiled again as she turned towards him, 'I'll take that as a compliment. It's fine. There's nothing wrong with expressing how you feel.'

Those words instantly put Karan at his ease, and he started talking as he normally would. The amazing thing was the easy and comfortable flow of their conversation, almost as if they were old friends. Shruti had had her reservations about deciding after just one meeting, but she instinctively felt that Karan was a good match and way better than any of the previous prospective grooms.

They had interacted a few times before, at family functions, but had never considered each other as potential life partners.

After a long conversation, Karan asked her, 'So, Shruti, what are your expectations from me? I need to ask you this if we're considering a future with each other.'

Seeing the seriousness on Karan's face, Shruti felt that this was probably the right moment to convey her feelings. However, she avoided eye contact because, on previous occasions, she had failed to evoke the right response, and she feared it would be the same this time as well. She didn't want to be disappointed again and hoped against hope for a positive closure to their meeting. Her silence bothered Karan. He thought of all the possible reasons for Shruti's aversion to taking things forward with this alliance. He strongly suspected that it was because he wasn't working with one of the reputed companies in the industry. However, he waited patiently for her to respond and say what was in her heart.

'I know that you work with a start-up, and I also know you understand what I might think about it.' The moment Shruti said this, Karan made up his mind. She was the one. If she could read his mind in such a short span of time, it had to be her.

'Everyone wants a guy who earns millions, and there's nothing wrong with that. I also understand that people can choose whom they want to spend their life with—in arranged marriages, you do have that option . . .'

Shruti interrupted him, 'I didn't mean that. In fact, I'm okay with it. For me, compatibility and honesty matter more than anything else. Moreover, you're doing well financially. Don't be offended, but I've done my research,' she grinned cheekily.

'Of course,' Karan said awkwardly, wondering whether he should be offended for having been stalked or be delighted that she had no problems about his work.

Shruti continued, 'I want to pursue a post-graduate degree in law after marriage. Currently, I am working in a law firm, but I have ambitions. However, my parents want me to marry first. I hope you are okay with that,' she had her fingers crossed.

'Why would I have a problem with it? It's good that you want to create your own identity.'

'I know . . . but not everyone thinks like that,' replied Shruti and then added, after a pause, 'also, I want to do it within a year of marriage because I've seen how difficult it is for people to get back into the groove of academics after they get caught up with the demands of marital life. I hope that won't be a problem because I won't be able to work and supplement your income while I'm focused on completing my postgrad. Therefore, while initially I may not be able to contribute to the household financially, trust me, it will be better for us in the long run.'

Karan thought about this for a second. He had hoped she would continue to work after they were married, but seeing her outlook towards her future and ambitions, he was convinced and confident that she was indeed the one he was looking for. A perfect blend of beauty and intelligence. He nodded, conceding to her plan to continue her studies and saw the relief and excitement on Shruti's face.

That night, after getting back home, Karan told his delighted parents that he was ready for marriage. The next morning, their parents talked with the panditji and the wedding date was set to be within two weeks' time.

Karan messaged Shruti after the date was confirmed, ending it with the heart emoticon:

So, 10 January 2020 it is. Are you happy? Before you ask me the same, let me tell you that I'm extremely happy and excited, but a little nervous too thinking about how our life will be. But I'm sure, with you by my side, it'll only get better. <3

Shruti was at her office when she read his message and smiled. Her colleagues, who were in the know, teased her gently. She had applied for leave as soon as the date was confirmed. She wanted to message Karan immediately but had waited for him to text her first so she could gauge his reaction.

She thought about what to say and then typed:

Yes, I'm equally happy, but have mixed feelings at present because it'll be a new world for me. Although I know you will treat me well, I still feel a gnawing anxiety. I really want a good life for both of us and trust me, I am already thinking about how our days together will be.

When Karan telephoned to tell me the good news, it came as a surprise. He had told me that he was going to 'see' a girl, but I had assumed he would wriggle out of it as he invariably did. I couldn't believe he was finally getting hitched, and that too in just a couple of weeks.

'Isn't it happening too fucking fast? Just two weeks? You should have at least taken some time to get to know her better.'

'Our parents thought that as we had both agreed to take this step, there was no point in delaying it. And I thought the same. I mean, it's not that getting married and sharing my space with some other person isn't scaring me, but how long could I have escaped it? Moreover, Shruti is a really nice girl.'

I kept teasing him over the phone until he asked, 'When is Jasmine coming from Delhi?'

'Tomorrow,' I replied.

'That's fantastic. At least she'll be of some help with my shopping and to arrange other things. You're useless anyway and would only add to the confusion.'

'Yeah right . . . now that you have a companion, why would you need my company? That's what happens, dude . . . not everyone is like me.'

'Are you done? If so, then let me call Jasmine and inform her. She'll be furious if I don't tell her the news myself.'

'Dude, I want to tell you something . . .' I still couldn't believe that Karan was getting married and wanted to laugh just thinking about it.

'Yeah, go on, tell me,' he said, expecting something serious.

'You know what . . . after a couple of weeks, by this time, *teri shaadi bhi khatam aur tu bhi khatam*,' I joked.

'Fuck you. Hang up.'

* * *

It is said that a successful marriage is falling in love with the same person over and over again, but to be honest, it is annoying the same person every single day, and yet, not giving up on each other. Jasmine and I had been married for three years, after a successful three-year long-distance relationship. We fought, we argued and had disagreements almost every day; but at the end of the day, we loved each other and felt warm in each other's company. I still remember how difficult it was for her to adapt to a whole new city as a newlywed. It's never easy for a girl to leave everything behind and start a new life, but Jasmine had carried the responsibility with ease, despite not understanding Marathi initially. Marriage is, indeed, not just the union of two souls; it's about years of growing together, along with each other's families, and the way she respected and loved my family made me love her even more. Even then, whenever she returned to Mumbai from her parents' house in Delhi, I eagerly looked forward to seeing her again, and would drive all the way to the airport to pick her up.

That day, my happiness had doubled, as not only was Jasmine returning home, but Karan was getting married. Luckily that day, I didn't get stuck in the rush-hour traffic in the evening and got to the airport early. I had texted Jasmine to check if she had landed but the message didn't get delivered.

I was waiting at a stall outside the airport, snacking on my favourite cheese frankie, when I received multiple

messages from Jasmine on WhatsApp. I guessed she had
sent them while she was still in the air, being equally
excited to see me after almost twenty days, but I was
baffled to read her texts:

*Aditya, I really love you, but please marry some nice girl.
Also, please take care of my family and always remember you
were my only love. I may not see you again, but somewhere
in heaven, I will really miss you. Love you, please take care of
yourself.*

I couldn't understand why she would send such
messages. I telephoned her as I drove towards the parking
area of the airport.

'What's the matter? I read your messages. Are you all
right?' I asked her.

'Don't ask. I thought the flight would crash today
with the heavy turbulence. Everyone in the aircraft was
terrified.'

I burst out laughing, thinking how crazy this girl
was to send such a desperate message. But she didn't
think it was funny at all and the more I laughed, the
angrier she got.

'I don't want to talk to you,' she snapped, deeply
annoyed.

'Okay.'

She didn't expect such a tame reply from me. 'Don't
you want to know the reason?'

'No. I trust your decision.' I was just teasing her as
I always loved to do. She disconnected the call. When
I got to the airport, I waited for Jasmine to collect her

luggage and emerge through the gate. My heart jumped for joy, seeing her after such a long gap.

The hypotheses that husbands enjoy greater freedom when the wife is away never held true for me. I loved her presence and was invariably happier when she was around, no matter what we were doing. We never placed any restrictions on each other, and hence had an inseparable bond. She smiled happily when she saw me, and I hugged her.

'This way,' I pointed to where I had parked the car and started walking in that direction.

Jasmine stared at me furiously, 'How selfish are you? Your wife has returned after such a hectic flight, and you are just walking away without offering to hold any bags?'

'Oh, my bad. Give one of those to me.' I turned to her and tried to take one of the two bags from her. But it was too late.

'Let it be. I'll carry it. Why don't such things come to you instinctively?'

It was better to keep my mouth shut. My apology would have irked her even more. That's how a husband's life is. I drove fifty kilometres and the gesture went unappreciated. Trust me, your wife can forgive you for her mistakes too.

We got into the car and after adjusting our seat belts, I said, 'So . . . Karan is finally getting married. Did you speak to him?'

She drank the juice I had bought for her, smiled and kissed my cheek. She loved me for the little things

I did but hated me more for all those little things that I didn't do.

'I did talk to Karan yesterday. But, as usual, it's going to be a boring Maharashtrian wedding without booze or non-veg. Why can't you guys booze openly like at our Punjabi weddings? You drink in the car outside the venue anyway.'

I laughed, 'I can't do anything about it, baby.'

On almost every alternate day for three years, we had held witty debates on Delhi versus Mumbai and Punjabis versus Maharashtrians, and there was still no clear winner.

* * *

I had tidied up, freshened up, ordered lunch online and just settled down to watch TV when my mobile phone rang. Jasmine had gone to bathe. It was my mom.

'When did you guys get home?' she demanded.

'About half an hour ago,' I replied.

'At least message me when you get home. I get worried.'

Mothers will be mothers, I sighed inwardly and replied, 'Okay, Mummy. We're home and I've ordered food because I'm hungry. Then, we'll eat our food, and after that, I have a couple of meetings . . .'

'Shut up,' she reacted and then asked, 'How's Jasmine? Is she okay?'

'Yeah, absolutely! Just that a little while ago, she wanted me to marry someone else.'

'Nonsense. Okay, bye.' She hung up. I couldn't understand why; I was only telling her the truth. I smiled and sent her a heart emoji. I knew she worried about me. It had been a year since we shifted into the new house we had bought. She always wanted to know if we had got home safely.

The bell rang. I was extremely hungry. I opened the door, hoping it would be the Zomato delivery boy, but no, it was Jasmine's online order, as always. By then, Jasmine had emerged from the room and was standing behind me. She could see my irritated face.

'It hasn't even been an hour since you got back, and your couriers have already started coming. For the last three weeks, there was complete peace—no couriers arriving one after the other.'

'Okay. I'm telling you beforehand, there are a few more. Most of them are essential things that we now need for Karan's wedding. Who's going to buy them? You?'

I wanted to bang my head on the wall, and she sensed that. I think every time she ordered something online, she prayed, 'Dear God, please don't let my husband be at home when these orders arrive.' But these little things only added a spark to our married life. It had been a long journey from a long-distance relationship to a long-lasting, trustworthy marriage.

Chapter 2

A month later, end of January

It had been two weeks since Karan and Shruti had joined the league of married couples. The wedding rituals were completed smoothly and Shruti was welcomed graciously into her new family by her in-laws. After returning from their honeymoon, they were relaxing at home after a really hectic fortnight. It was Sunday, and both Karan and she were to resume work the next day.

'I'm still hungover from Himachal. I just wish we could have stayed there for a few more days and had at least another week off,' Shruti said plaintively.

'We can just stay in our room for one more week, without doing any work. Sound good?' Karan asked, brushing his lips against hers.

'Yeah, why not? And the bills will be paid by our parents, right? What an awesome plan!' Shruti replied sarcastically.

Karan shrugged with a mischievous glint in his eyes, 'Is it my fault that I want to spend time with my beautiful wife?'

Shruti pushed past him, hearing Karan's mother calling them to say she needed Karan to take her to the dentist for her root canal treatment. She told Shruti that a few close relatives were coming over for lunch. That was when Shruti decided that she would cook for everyone and give Karan a surprise too. She hadn't done any cooking after her wedding as, being a new bride, she had not been allowed into the kitchen. When they both left, Shruti consulted Karan's father, who was busy fiddling with his phone.

'Papa, I want to make the dessert today. May I?'

Karan's father set his phone aside and looked up. 'Are you sure?' he asked. Although Shruti nodded enthusiastically, Karan's father said, 'But you need to prepare for that case that your firm asked you to work on. Also, you don't need to exhaust yourself after your tiring trip.'

'No, trust me. I can manage it.' Shruti was very keen and set about convincing her father-in-law to let her into the kitchen.

'But I don't know the traditional customs to introduce you to the kitchen. Wasn't Karan's mother saying something about it last night?'

'I've cleared it with my mummy and there shouldn't be any problem. Also, Karan's uncles are coming today, along with their families, and I thought I could at least prepare a sweet dish for all of us.'

'Did you tell Karan about it?' he asked.

'No. I want to give both Aai and Karan a surprise.'

Karan's father didn't want her to be put to so much trouble as everything was still very new to her, but on the inside, he was delighted to hear her words and see her enthusiasm. It revealed her as a family-oriented homemaker, while her dedication to her career reflected her independence and intelligence. Although it had only been a few days, even during the trip, she had never failed to call them and interact with them at least once a day. Her caring nature was very obvious. He felt very proud of himself, feeling he couldn't have found a better girl for Karan.

'Okay, I'll help you. Let's make halwa,' he said, being a dab hand in the kitchen himself.

Shruti had never made halwa before. She looked for a YouTube video, and her mother, who was equally excited about her cooking for the first time at her in-laws' house, also gave her a few instructions.

Shruti's hands ached as she struggled to grate the carrots. Karan's father, as he set about preparing the rest of the lunch, noticed her determinedly grappling with the grater. After an almost hour-long battle, she triumphantly completed the task. She wanted to finish her maiden voyage in the kitchen before Karan and her mother-in-law returned, but time was running out. Karan's father patiently guided her through the larder where the ghee and dry fruits were stored. At long last, the halwa was ready. Shruti clicked a photograph of it and WhatsApped it to her mother, who was content to just look at it, although she couldn't taste it.

'Will you try some?' she asked her father-in-law.

There was no way he could deny tasting the first fruits of his daughter-in-law's labour. More so when its aroma was so tempting. He took a bite and closed his eyes savouring it as it melted in his mouth, satisfying his taste buds like never before.

'Were you lying about this being your first time?' he demanded. Shruti looked at him confused and a little worried, a question in her eyes. He smiled and added, 'This is simply delicious. I was fed up of the boring desserts that Karan's mother makes. Thank God, I won't have to eat boring halwa any more. Trust me, everyone is going to lick their bowls clean.'

Shruti was delighted to hear the appreciation, 'Thank you, Papa.'

She put the halwa in the fridge to set and cleared the mess on the kitchen counter as soon as Karan's dad was done preparing the lunch. By the time Karan and his mother returned, their relatives had joined them. After all their praise for the lovely wedding ceremony and other casual talk, Karan's mother laid the table, although she had been advised to rest after the dental procedure.

Karan's father and Shruti exchanged conspiratorial grins as her mother-in-law brought in the dessert. Shruti took the bowl and ladled out the halwa. They hadn't yet revealed that it had been made by her. It was only when everyone praised the dish that Karan's father said, 'Isn't it one of the best halwas you've had in years?'

Karan's uncle took another bite and said, 'Bhaiya, not one of the best—it's the best! How did you become such an excellent chef?'

'The credit doesn't go to me for this.' He glanced at Shruti, who blushed.

'Did you make it?' Karan asked, looking at her sparkling eyes as she served it to him.

She didn't say a word, simply nodded and smiled. Karan and his mother were pleasantly surprised by her gesture. Karan's mother kissed her forehead affectionately and went 'into her bedroom.' When she returned, she was holding a *shagun*, a gift envelope, and gave it to Shruti, who devoutly touched her mother-in-law's feet before accepting it.

'*Bhabhi*, you're truly blessed to have her as a daughter-in-law,' said Karan's *chachi*.

Karan swelled with pride and whispered in Shruti's ears, 'It's yummy.'

Karan's chachi, who was sitting beside him, chided Karan, 'Why are you eating alone? Feed her first.'

Everyone cheered as Karan brought the spoon to her mouth and fed her. Shruti smiled at him coyly. After everyone had left, when Karan and Shruti were alone in their room, Karan confessed that he had wanted to have a second helping of the dessert, but it had all been gone before he could reach for the bowl.

Shruti left the room and returned a few moments later with the small extra bowl of dessert which she had kept aside especially for Karan. His eyes glittered with emotion at Shruti's thoughtfulness. As she fed him with love, Karan gently drew her on to his lap.

'I love you, Shruti. I'm really, really happy that I have you in my life forever. Thank you for what you did today. It means a lot to me.'

'Did you like it?' she caressed his cheek.

'Of course. Not just me; Mummy loved it too. I could see the pride and joy in her eyes. They were right, I couldn't have found anyone better.'

'So, what do I get in return now?' she asked playfully.

'You'll know it soon.' He kissed her and made her get off from his lap so he could pick his laptop. In that moment, Karan had decided the plan, but needed to shoot off some urgent office emails first. Shruti sat beside him on the bed, idly checking her Instagram feed. In a couple of hours, when he was done with all the office calls and emails, he told Shruti to get ready as he planned to take her out for the evening. Shruti was excited. She got ready in no time and Karan changed into a blue shirt which Shruti loved to see him in.

Shruti had slipped into a slinky black dress which took Karan's breath away. 'You are so beautiful, my love! I promise to make tonight a night to remember.'

Shruti smiled as, hand in hand, they walked out of their house.

'At least tell me where we are going,' Shruti said as the car moved swiftly along the Western Express Highway.

'To one of your favourite places, for one of your favourite dishes. I remember you mentioning it to me once,' Karan turned to her when he stopped at a traffic light. 'I can't give you any more hints.'

He gently intertwined his fingers with hers. Shruti watched, smiling, as he struggled to retain her warm clasp and simultaneously change gears. She loved the way he showed his affection and helped him hold her hand as he should have. She was still wondering about their mystery destination as the streets flashed past.

'Is it Pal's Fish Corner in Bandra?'

'Not even close.' Karan laughed.

Shruti then sat back and pretended to enjoy the moment and their drive. After a few minutes, she asked Karan for his phone to take a picture of them. Karan gave his phone to her, and she clicked a few selfies. When his attention was wholly absorbed by the traffic on the road, Shruti clicked open his Google Maps and checked the last location he had searched for. Karan would have looked up the time required to get there. And voilà! There it was.

'Sidhivinayak Pav Bhaji at Juhu Chowpatty!' she sang out joyfully and returned his phone.

Karan understood that she had outwitted him. 'I don't know whether I should call that smart or over smart,' he grumbled good-naturedly, 'Anyway, although the place is right, there's a lot more to it.'

Although this had been her favourite haunt on weekends, to unwind, watching the sunset and tucking into her favourite pav bhaji, she couldn't quite understand how Karan planned to make this evening all that special.

Earlier that afternoon, Karan had had a word with the owner of Sidhivinayak to ask his permission before asking a local decorator to set a table with flowers and lights.

Shruti's eyes filled with tears. She hadn't expected her husband to go to such lengths to make her feel loved.

She kissed him passionately right there on the street. She realized that they were indulging in the infamous PDA (severely frowned upon in their society) and hurriedly broke off the kiss. Karan, a bit embarrassed, looked around sheepishly, although he had enjoyed Shruti's exuberant response to his surprise.

They sat down to indulge in their favourite Mumbai cuisine with an unrivalled view of the sunset.

* * *

It is said that friendship takes a backseat when someone in the group gets married. Although I have seen this phenomenon, it never held true for Karan and me. Our equation didn't change a bit.

Furthermore, Jasmine and Shruti bonded extremely well over the past month, and we couldn't have asked for anything more. Half of your marital problems are resolved if you gel well with each other's social circle.

One of the few people who was still a bachelor in our group was Neerav and we never missed an opportunity to tease him about it. It was 19 February, and Jasmine, along with Karan, Shruti and Neerav, had planned a trip to Goa in the following week, to celebrate my birthday. This has been an annual pilgrimage of sorts ever since the beginning of our friendship. With each visit, we discovered something new; the city's energy blew our mind. This year, it had been a last-minute decision because Karan hadn't been granted leave. We had booked train tickets so it wouldn't be a huge loss if we weren't able to make it. Unfortunately, the trip felt jinxed right from the start and something or the other came up to ruin our meticulous plans.

This time, just when it looked like everything would smoothly fall into place—with the train tickets and hotel booked—Neerav's grandfather fell ill and was rushed to the hospital. Being very close to Neerav, I was upset, because the Goa trip wouldn't be the same if he were to drop out.

'I just hope Neerav is able to make it,' I said, when Jasmine and I were having dinner at home.

'Don't worry,' said Jasmine, cheerfully. 'Nothing will happen to his grandfather. He'll be discharged before we leave for Goa on 24 January, and we'll all go to Thalassa.' I couldn't help smiling at her optimism.

Unfortunately, Neerav's grandfather's condition deteriorated rapidly. Eventually, a day prior to our scheduled day of travel, the old man passed away. To be honest, I wasn't sure whether I was sad that he had lost a loved one or sorry that our hopes of his joining the trip had been dashed. But his folks needed him. I telephoned him and told him to take care of his family and himself, and then called Karan.

'Yeah, I know, he texted me too. I really didn't think his grandfather's condition was this critical,' said Karan.

'It wasn't, initially, but the complications compounded. At that age, the body slowly stops reacting to treatments.'

'Sad,' said Karan. 'What should we do now?'

I thought for a second and said, 'Let's stick to our plan.' I didn't want to ruin Jasmine's plans and anyway, the bookings had already been made.

So, as per our original schedule, one day before my birthday, the four of us landed in Goa and checked in into our hotel on Candolim Road. We had adjacent rooms and decided to freshen up and then meet up in a couple of hours.

Shruti unpacked her bags and changed into her pyjamas while Karan smoked in the balcony. She went out and stood beside him.

Resting her head on his shoulder, she said, 'Did you know that this is my first time in Goa?'

Karan discarded his cigarette butt in the ashtray and looked at Shruti in disbelief. 'Really? In all these years, you've never been to Goa? Not even with family?'

'I did come once when I was a child with my family, but that's it.'

'Wow, that's unbelievable!' Karan took her in his arms and reassured her, 'Don't worry, we'll party hard and make up for all your lost time.'

'Sure. I'm really tired right now after the long train journey. I'll take a nap. Unless you need something,' Shruti went back into the room and Karan followed her.

'No, you go to sleep. I'll just sit here and watch you,' said Karan cheekily.

'Can I ask you something which has been on my mind since day one?' Shruti asked as she prepared her bed, moving the pillows and duvet around.

'Yes, sure.' Karan perched on the other side of the bed.

'Why did you say yes to me? I mean, what did you see in me when we met? And please don't say I looked beautiful and stupid things like that,' Shruti rolled over to sit beside Karan.

'But, come on, you are beautiful,' Karan protested.

'There must be something else that you saw in me. Did you say yes only because you thought I was beautiful?'

Karan drew her close, 'It's because you were able to read my mind with ease.'

Shruti raised her eyebrows, wondering what he meant. 'And what did I read correctly?'

'Nothing, go to sleep. There are some things that are not meant to be said.'

He caressed her forehead lovingly and covered her face with tiny butterfly kisses to make her go to sleep. Shruti dozed off instantly with her head on his chest. Karan watched her, enchanted by his very own sleeping beauty.

After resting for a while, Karan telephoned me and asked me to join him by the pool for a pint of beer. Jasmine was fast asleep. I locked the door and went out without disturbing her. When I went down, I was surprised to see a sea of girls in the pool. Karan, sitting at a poolside table, was the only guy I could see. I walked over to him and asked him what the fuck was happening.

'It's a college trip. They are from Chandigarh,' he replied. 'Stunned to see so many good-looking girls, I asked the waiter who they were.'

'Is that the reason you called me downstairs? Asshole, you're married now. Stop ogling them!'

'Fuck you. Just because I have diabetes doesn't mean I cannot take pleasure in sniffing the chocolate.' Karan winked and opened the pint bottle for me.

'You're incorrigible. Anyways, cheers.' I had a sip of the beer and posted a photograph on Instagram. We were just chatting when one of the hotel staff approached us.

'Is there a problem?' I asked, seeing him hesitate near our table, clearly unwilling to intrude on our conversation.

'Sir, this is a private party here. Will you please shift to the bar?'

What the fuck! Does he think we're sitting here to see girls in swimsuits? Seeing my expression darken, he immediately read my mind.

'Sirji,' I said, keeping a tight lid on my temper, 'if you think we're here for the girls, you're sadly mistaken. We're waiting for wives to join us. They're coming down in a few minutes.'

He didn't say anything and left. A few minutes later, I saw their professor discussing something with the manager, throwing meaningful glances at us. This was seriously pissing me off, so I called Jasmine to let her know what was happening.

Within a few minutes, she came down along with Shruti, and both the girls pounced on the manager. 'Yes, what's the problem?'

'What is it, ma'am?' he asked, not knowing what they meant. The college professor could hear their exchange.

Jasmine was seething and it was evident in her tone, 'You say there's a private party here; have they booked the entire hotel or just the pool area? If so, why weren't we informed when we checked in that the pool area wasn't accessible? If we're staying here in this hotel, then we have the right to access the pool.'

Jasmine paused for breath and Shruti interjected, 'As guests of this hotel, no one can refuse us access to the pool just because there's another group here.'

We had to literally peel our wives away and push them into the pool to cool them down. Who would have dared to stop us after that? We, too, jumped into the pool and had a blast with our drinks for the next few hours. After we got tired of dancing and playing in the water, Karan and I sat at the edge of the pool and sipped our beers.

Our wives came over to us. Jasmine had a mischievous smile on her face as she turned to Shruti and said, 'See, at the end of the day, wives had to come to the rescue of their husbands.'

'Of course, we are the bosses anyway.' Shruti's shrug would've put a Mafioso in the shade.

Karan was about to protest, but I forestalled him. 'Bro, get used to it. This is just the beginning. The most important words after marriage aren't "I love you"; they're "it's my fault" and "I'm sorry".'

We all laughed. It was good to see Jasmine letting her hair down and really enjoying herself. Nothing in this world meant more than her happiness to me.

* * *

The next day, we woke up late after the all-night, pre-birthday bash. When I opened my eyes, Jasmine was already holding the huge bouquet of flowers that she'd had custom-made for me with my initials. Even our bedroom had been decorated with balloons. I had been so dead drunk that I'd had no clue when she did all this. I was amazed, and still in bed, when Jasmine came over and kissed me.

'Happy birthday, my love. May all your wishes come true this year,' she said.

'Thank you. I love you, so much. When did you manage to do all this?' I asked curiously, getting up.

'Shruti helped me inflate the balloons in the morning and the hotel staff arranged for the bouquet.' Jasmine smiled. She opened a pastry box and fed me my favourite red velvet cake. There was something about our relationship that I couldn't express in words, but the way she never failed to amaze me every year with little surprises warmed my heart. Sometimes, I looked at her and just felt incredibly lucky to have her; but I didn't say this enough. Somehow, I knew she already knew it. Happiness in marriage is not something that just happens. It is created by putting in lot of effort every day; by doing these little things.

I checked my mobile to see many missed calls and birthday messages. I scrolled down to see if Neerav had messaged or called but there was not a single notification from him. I told Jasmine that I was worried that I hadn't heard from Neerav.

'He must be with his grieving family. All the relatives would have come to mourn. He'll call as soon as he's free,' Jasmine assured me, and I nodded in agreement. However, I still felt a bit worried about his silence.

After freshening up, we had breakfast in our rooms in luxury and then all four of us got ready and rode the hired Activas to Thalassa, where Jasmine had pre-booked a table. She knew that it was one of my most favourite places in Goa. When I walked into the café, I couldn't believe my eyes when I saw a carbon copy of Neerav standing by the table at the far end, near the water.

Am I still hungover? I wondered.

'Doesn't that guy look exactly like Neerav?' I whispered to Jasmine.

Her reply came as a pleasant surprise, 'He doesn't just "look like" Neerav, he is Neerav.'

'What? When did he arrive in Goa?' my jaw dropped in disbelief.

'Just now. That's why he didn't call you, as he was in the train, and you would have guessed it easily.'

'So, you guys knew?' I asked Karan.

'Yup,' Karan grinned, 'he told us yesterday that he was boarding the late-night train after completing all the funeral rituals. We wanted to surprise you.'

I wanted to yell abusive words at everyone in Hindi, which I eventually did too. He hadn't checked in yet and had his luggage with him. He thought he would miss the moment if he went to the hotel first and then drove down to Thalassa. As soon as he saw me, he popped open a bottle of champagne and sang the song, *'Ek teri yaari ka hi saaton janam haqdaar hoon main . . . Tera yaar hoon main.'* Although I was over the moon to see him, I pretended to be pissed off at all this subterfuge.

He laughed and said, 'How could I not come to my brother's birthday? I had to, obviously; and that too when I'm getting free booze in Goa.'

I punched his chest and called him a dumbass. We both laughed and embraced each other affectionately. It was not like we had been in college together or shared the same profession, but when we met through a mutual friend half a decade ago, we instantly knew that we would be friends forever. Now, five years later, not only did he share a bond with me, but also with Jasmine. We would sit talking into the wee hours of the night about anything and everything under the sun.

That was what made our friendship special because our level of craziness was a perfect match. Jasmine even called us twins. And with his presence, my birthday night turned into one hell of a crazy ride.

Chapter 3

'How's everyone at home?' I asked Neerav.

It was the next day, and the three of us were strolling around the town. Jasmine and Shruti had set out on a shopping spree by themselves because we were not interested in scouring shop after shop for God alone knew what.

'Dad had a bit of a breakdown after Grandpa passed away. However, as everyone, including Dad, had been mentally prepared for it, Dad eventually managed to pull himself together. Dad had been aware of the agony Grandpa had been going through in the past few months.'

'It's a blessing that he has finally been relieved of that. May his soul rest in peace,' said Karan.

'Yeah. As soon as the funeral rituals were done, both Mom and Dad told me that I could come and join you guys, so here I am,' Neerav stretched himself to relieve his backache. 'For the last few days, what with the continuous hospital visits, I've developed a bad body ache. I need to get a nice massage.'

I grinned mischievously and said, 'Why not? You're in Goa, where else would you get a good massage?'

'You guys are crazy. Neerav still has a licence for that, but we don't,' Karan instantly reacted, frowning at me.

'Bhai, we're talking about a normal professional massage, nothing else—,' I began.

Neerav interrupted, '—and especially in Goa where there's a huge chance that you'll get looted.'

'I'm not coming,' Karan declared as we walked back towards the hotel.

Neerav started pulling his leg, saying, 'I told you he'll change after marriage. From now on, he'll first take permission from Shruti for everything he does.'

'It's not that. I don't know what Shruti would think if I told her that I'm going to a massage parlour. But you guys should go.'

'You're already turning into one of those henpecked husbands.' This time it was me teasing him.

'I'll tell Jasmine and then we'll see which one of us is fucking henpecked!' he retorted.

'Jasmine already knows. I never do anything secretly. She knows I won't cross my limits.'

However, Karan refused to give in despite our best effort to convince him, so eventually, Neerav and I decided to go. We googled for a good professional parlour, one that had good ratings, and shortlisted one. We followed the map to a deserted road. I was sitting on the back of the Activa he was driving. Looking around, I could only see dodgy and rundown lodges in a derelict neighbourhood; half of these seemed to be non-operational.

'This looks fishy,' I told Neerav, looking around when we finally reached the place.

"Did you give me the right directions?" he asked.

'Of course. Shall we look for some better parlours?'

I rechecked to see if we were at the right place, and we were. The photos on Google were misleading, to say the least; in reality, it was a far cry from the classy establishment depicted on the website. There were some guys who looked like bouncers standing outside and some staff, publicizing their services with pamphlets in their hands. Neerav parked the Activa at a distance and had a look at the parlour.

'No worries, nothing will happen. Let's go,' he said and crossed the road.

I wasn't entirely convinced, but followed him, placing my trust in his instinct. We were greeted pleasantly, which was unexpected, and politely asked which of their massages we wanted.

'We provide all kinds of services: B2B, happy ending and so on. What would you prefer?' the bouncer asked.

I had a sinking feeling that we were going to get right royally fucked today and whispered my misgivings to Neerav.

Neerav 'was too busy poring through the flyer in his hand to hear me'. 'We just want a normal massage. No special services,' he told the bouncer.

'Okay, sir, please follow me.' He guided us through a narrow passage that took us to a counter that looked even more suspicious. He whispered into the ear of the person at the counter, who looked like the manager.

'Please wait for five minutes,' the manager gestured to sit on the couch.

It was getting creepier than a cheap thriller. I had been to many sophisticated spas before so this level of tawdriness was a first for me. Neerav sat down calmly but I could tell that he was shit scared inside.

'Do you really think we should go ahead with this?' I asked nervously.

'Don't overreact. We've asked for a normal service.' His response to me seemed more like reassurance for himself that nothing would go wrong.

After a few minutes, a couple of good-looking girls welcomed us and took us to our respective cabins. The lady who took charge of me asked me to change and I lay face down on the massage bed in a towel. She started working on my legs. It was so relaxing. All my tiredness evaporated. She must've been an expert, because within a few minutes, I fell asleep. I woke up only when she asked me to turn over and I realized all my pain had vanished. I asked her why she hadn't woken me up and she smiled and said that she wanted me to relax. She then massaged my upper body and I felt rejuvenated.

As soon as she was done, I thanked her politely and admitted, 'At first I had my doubts, thinking it would be a horrible experience here, but you were amazingly professional. I feel so good now.'

'Thank you, sir. I hope you'll visit again.'

I smiled and walked out, feeling relaxed and energetic. Neerav too had come out by then and had a big smile on his face. We realized that our fears had been groundless, and it had actually been a good experience—or so we thought, until we got back to our hotel and Neerav discovered that all the cash from his wallet was missing.

'Why didn't you check it there?' I asked, as he hurriedly checked his other pockets to see if he had inadvertently put his money in one of them.

'I felt so relaxed as soon as it was all done, and I actually thought that she was pretty decent because not once did she try to solicit for any extra services. Fuck, man, I shouldn't have carried cash with me.'

Damn, and here I had been thinking about giving the masseuse a tip for making me feel so good.

'Are you sure you were carrying the cash along with you? You should check your room too,' I said.

'No, I'm sure I had it in my wallet. Around twenty-five hundred rupees.'

'There's no point in going back and asking for it. They'll just deny that they had anything to do with you losing your money,' I said. Now that we couldn't do anything about it, and what was done was done, I ribbed him playfully, 'You must've asked for those special services; don't lie. I swear I won't tell anyone. Which one did you opt for? Happy ending or full service?'

'That's the whole fuckin' point! I'm not sad because I lost twenty-five hundred rupees, but because the massage cost me around four thousand rupees. Forget happy endings, I didn't even get to do anything. How tragic is that?'

We both laughed hysterically just thinking about the incident. Neerav had a wry sense of humour and would find a way to laugh and stay happy even in the face of the worst tragedies.

'Now, for God's sake, don't tell anyone. Jasmine will harass me for the rest of my life if she were to get wind of this fiasco. She already has so many drunken videos of me.'

'Sorry, buddy, after half a bottle down, that's beyond my control.'

* * *

We enjoyed Goa to the fullest for the next couple of days and then returned to Mumbai. Karan, Shruti and Neerav got back to their work immediately despite their Goa hangover. Shruti decided to start studying for her post-graduation. She had already put in her resignation and only had to complete the formalities of working through her notice period in the office. Both Karan and Neerav were anticipating salary hikes, considering their excellent performance in the previous year. As Jasmine planned to resume work at her office the next day, we decided to visit my parents, as we couldn't do so on my birthday.

'So, are you getting back to work tomorrow?' Mom asked Jasmine.

'Yes. I wish we could've had a few days more in Goa,' Jasmine replied wistfully.

'It looks like you guys are mentally always in Goa,' Mom said teasingly and then, on a more serious note, 'and once again, you'll have to get up at five in the morning and get ready to catch the bus at six, right? How do you manage that and handle the household simultaneously? I'm sure Aditya does nothing to help you with the daily chores.'

'No ... no ... he does a lot of work,' Jasmine valiantly defended me. I didn't know whether she was being sarcastic or really meant it. In any case, it felt good.

'Good, at least he's learning now.' This was my dad butting in. I preferred to hold my peace during these discussions and listen to their nonsense, because I knew they loved me and such leg-pulling was merely routine when we were all together.

After dinner, we were just sitting around, when Mom said, 'Now that a new year has started in your life, you both should think of planning a family. I'll retire in a couple of years and can take care of the baby.'

'And who'll look after the child in the first two years?' I said to lighten the mood. However, Mom was on her favourite hobby horse now and refused to be diverted. She continued bombarding us with questions, one after the other. It's extremely difficult to cope with these questions after a few years of marriage. It's like that's the only goal after marriage.

I thought about ways and means to tactfully extricate Jasmine and me from this uncomfortable discussion and continued, 'We've only just shifted to our new house, Mummy. We've been staying with you for all these years; we still need time to learn to juggle the daily household activities and our careers now that we live independently.'

'I know that. And we're happy and very proud that both of you have managed to take on this responsibility. What more could we want as parents?' she replied.

'Apart from giving you a grandchild,' I laughed, but my laughter died down when I glanced at Jasmine, looking downright miserable, and realized that the discussion had turned sour. She felt cornered and fell silent, whenever such topics came up. She couldn't even react the way I did and laugh it off, as they were her in-laws after all, even if they treated her like a daughter.

After a brief pause, Mom said, 'Do you realize that after a year or so, people will start asking questions?'

I got up from the couch and sat beside her. 'Mom, when did you start taking people's opinions seriously? Do you remember they told you to not let me become a writer? Even now, they're nosey about why we shifted to a new house when we live so close. Was it your daughter-in-law's idea to set up her own household and blah blah?'

'That's different. I don't give a damn about those things. In fact, I give as good as I get when I hear such nonsense and tell these busybodies that we are very proud that you've bought your own place. Your dad bought a house when he was your age, so that's as it should be. I think they're just jealous because Jasmine and I get along well and don't have a typical *saas–bahu* relationship. What I'm driving at concerns only you two and no one else. Your daily routine and work will never end. But this is the right age.'

'Okay, Mom, we'll think it over.' I didn't want to prolong this excruciating discussion any further and this was the only way to end it.

My dad decided to step in and defuse the uncomfortable situation, so he interrupted with, 'It's getting too hot here. Anyone wants a beer?'

'I'll bring it. You sit,' I said when I saw him getting up to go into the kitchen.

'Jasmine, you want?' Dad asked her.

'No, Papa. I already had enough,' she replied.

I fervently hoped that she meant she'd had enough beer in Goa and not the discussion that had taken place a few minutes ago. If not, I would be in deep shit at home. But she did mean the former and hit the sack as soon as we got home because she had to wake up early the next day.

In the morning, when she woke me up before leaving, I noticed she looked dull. I got up immediately and asked her if she was okay.

'Yeah, I am fine. Don't worry,' she replied, but her voice was heavy.

'I'm pretty sure you're lying and won't tell me how you're truly feeling.' I was right. She had a fever. I set her bag aside and made her sit down.

'Is it absolutely necessary to go in to work today? You're not well and the two-hour commute will only make you feel worse. Just tell your HR that you won't be coming today.'

'No, trust me . . . I'm fine. If I were feeling weak, I would've applied for leave. Don't worry and eat your lunch on time.' She kissed me goodbye before I could convince her any further.

That was just the way she was. I loved the way she took care of me, my family and our house, along with her demanding job; but hated the way she neglected her health in the bargain. I was truly blessed to have a wife like her; a person who knew how to maintain relationships and nurture them with love.

* * *

'You know, Karan, I always wanted to live a life like this,' said Shruti. As they exited the theatre after watching a movie at Viviana Mall, she affectionately linked her arm through his. Their house was merely half a kilometre away from the mall and they had preferred to walk rather than drive.

'Like what?' Karan asked. 'Walking because petrol is getting costlier day by day?' he laughed, casting a sidelong glance at Shruti.

'Shut up. Don't be so unromantic,' she pinched his arm. 'Like watching late-night movies with my husband, followed by a romantic walk back to our home, where I can share my deepest thoughts and express whatever I feel without any fear of judgement.' She looked up at him, blushing.

'That was deep,' Karan stated. 'So, am I living up to your expectations or not?'

He looked at her curiously. Shruti pretended to ponder and then answered, 'Ummm . . . you could say that.'

'Then how much would you rate me?' Karan took it a step further.

'Eight,' replied Shruti instantly, almost as if she had already thought about it.

'That was too quick. You should reconsider.'

'No, that's final.'

'And why, may I ask, did you cut those two points?' Karan asked seriously. It was already midnight, and they were at the gates of their society complex. 'Oh, come on. Don't be a typical husband. You've passed with distinction.' Shruti laughed in reply.

'Okay, my princess,' Karan kissed her hand and then said, 'but I would rate you a seven.'

Shruti grinned and looked at Karan, 'Now why's that?'

'One point less than me because you're leaving me alone tomorrow and going to your parents' home . . . and I'm going to miss you.'

Shruti cupped his cheeks. 'I'll miss you too. But I need to go. Papa isn't well and Mom won't be able to handle him alone. Also, I haven't gone home since the wedding.'

'Obviously, you should go,' Karan stated as he opened the elevator door. 'I am not stopping you. I've got so used to having you around that it's going to be difficult. I'll feel very lonely in our room without you. I love when you're by my side.'

'I'll always be by your side. I love you and I'll miss you too. Promise me you'll take care of yourself and not overwork or get stressed out.'

'Don't worry, I will.'

As soon as they were in their room, Karan drew Shruti close. She could see the passion in his eyes and decided that she no longer wanted to wait. She closed her eyes. She could hear him breathe and felt his face near hers. At first, it was just a gentle, feathering kiss on her lips, but it soon turned passionate. She tangled her fingers in his hair, caressing his neck because she felt the urge to pull him even closer. The bristles of his beard scratched her soft cheeks as she gripped his head firmly, as if she were trying to stop him from eluding her caresses. He kissed her the way she wanted to be kissed, not trying to win a battle but seeking union and closeness and sharing a timeless and passionate moment.

The next morning, Shruti made sure to fix breakfast for everybody before she left. She also helped Karan get ready for work, as he was supposed to leave early. Karan packed his laptop and the documents he needed for his presentation and came into the dining room for his breakfast. His parents were already having the French toast that Shruti had made. She loved cooking whatever she knew, and Karan's parents loved whatever she made. As soon as Karan was seated at the dining table, she placed a plate of toast in front of him.

'At what time are you leaving to drop her off?' asked his mother.

'I'm going directly to office. Shruti will take a cab,' Karan replied, munching busily.

'Aren't you dropping her off?' his mother's voice had risen by several octaves. 'She's going home for the first time, Karan, and you're letting her go by cab? How inconsiderate is that?' his mother was obviously deeply disappointed.

'What's the big deal? I'm late for work and Shruti said that she would go by cab,' Karan defended himself.

'Obviously, she'll say that. When a girl goes home for the first time after her wedding, it's traditional for the husband to accompany her. Customs aside, her parents would feel happy to see you both together.'

Shruti overheard their conversation from the kitchen and when she came out with the last few slices of French toast, she said, 'Aai, it's fine. There's no need for such formalities. Also, Karan has an important meeting today. Let him go. I'll manage.'

Karan loved the way she supported his decision, knowing that he had a crucial meeting. After breakfast, he went into their bedroom and called Shruti. He wanted to hug her one last time before she left. Shruti knew it and shyly followed him in, excusing herself.

'What? Do you think Aai and Papa won't know why you've called me inside?' Shruti chided as she stepped into the bedroom and Karan closed the door behind her.

'So what? As if they've never gone through this phase.' He wrapped his arms around her and planted a kiss on her lips. 'Miss me!' he commanded. The sadness of being away from Shruti was evident on his face.

Shruti hugged him again and said, 'Now, leave. You're already late.'

'Are you planning to get rid of me so soon? I won't let that happen.' Karan winked at her.

'Shut up. Bye.' She opened the door and pushed him out.

'Love you, too,' he replied, reading her mind.

In a very short span, they had discovered that they were indeed soulmates. She wasn't really homesick for her parents. She took care of all the little things Karan needed, and in return, he showered her with all the love in his heart.

Later that afternoon, after Shruti's work formalities were finalized, she had a nice chat with her parents, went up to her old bedroom and then decided to take a shower. After the shower, she changed into loose clothes and sat on her bed with her mobile phone.

She decided to text Karan, despite knowing it was a busy day for him: 'Do you have some time for your wife? She's missing you.'

Karan didn't take long to reply and her phone promptly vibrated: 'Just got done with the meeting; didn't have my lunch yet. But I'll always have time for you, my love. I miss you too. How're Mom and Dad?'

Shruti smiled at his response and then replied, 'They're fine. But why haven't you had your lunch yet? First eat and then talk.'

The way they had built their relationship was adorable. Their arranged marriage didn't feel arranged any more.

Chapter 4

It had been a week since Shruti had gone to her parents' home, and Karan was saddened by the fact that every night that he spent away from her was a night they would never have together. Who says husbands don't miss their wives when they're away? Karan missed her terribly and the desire to be around her flared up.

Shruti's mind also dwelled on Karan most of the day. They would have long telephone conversations at night and whenever possible during the day. She would send him texts for no reason at all, but she also kept busy with her usual routine and studies, and relaxed, spending less effort on her appearance, and having informal eat-when-she-wanted meals instead of sit-down-with-the-family meals. Her father had recovered and she, along with her parents, was scheduled to go to Pune for a family function for a few days. When Karan got to know about it that morning, his entire day at work went dull and lacklustre. He eventually called Shruti, and she promptly answered it after just one ring.

'Were you expecting my call?' Karan had a huge smile on his face.

'I knew you would call. My instincts are strong, you know that.'

'You missed your calling. You should have been in the police force rather than a PG in law,' Karan mocked her.

'Funny,' said Shruti, sarcastically. 'We're leaving tonight. Some of our other relatives are joining us and Dad has booked a minibus. You should've also come along.'

'You know appraisals are around the corner. Else, I would've.'

Shruti wanted him to come. It would have been their first family function together. Her eyes filled with tears, but she understood Karan's situation too. She picked up their wedding photograph from the bedside table and her sadness transformed into joy.

'Why are you smiling?' Karan asked curiously as he heard her giggling.

'You look so funny in this picture from our wedding reception; almost as if you're feeding me against your will.'

'I was dead tired after clicking photographs with more than five hundred guests,' grumbled Karan, although he couldn't help smiling too. 'I miss you. When are you planning to return?'

'I'll be back within a week, around 27 March, and then we'll be together. I'll take you out on a dinner date to your favourite place this time.'

Karan counted the number of days on the calendar in front of him and sighed. 'What am I supposed to do until then? This week I don't even have much to do because my workload has suddenly reduced because of some virus going around.'

'What virus are you talking about?'

'Haven't you seen the news? There's a bug called Corona that's spreading rapidly. Since the past few days, clients are reluctant to attend meetings.'

'Really? I haven't watched the news for quite some time now. Is it serious?'

'I don't think so. I think it's just a hoax or some political stunt to dent the economy again. In any case, it's the common man, like me, who'll pay the price.'

'You're not "common". You're special . . . to me,' cooed Shruti.

'You're also special . . . to me. Please take care of yourself. I'll see you soon.'

After Karan hung up, he got busy with the scheduled calls and his tasks for the day. When he got home, he saw his parents poring through the marriage album that had been delivered in the afternoon. They were so engrossed that they didn't realize he was home. He decided not to disturb them and immediately took out the phone from his pocket to message Shruti.

I just came home. Guess what? Our marriage album has arrived. Now, in your absence, I can at least relive our marriage memories. I didn't tell you, but every day, I look forward to sharing my thoughts, my ideas, my mood swings, my disappointments, my office issues and everything else with you. I just need to look into your eyes and know that no matter how the world is spinning, things are all right because you love me so much.

Shruti read the message and replied,

To be with you . . . that's all I want. And I'll be home soon and in your arms.

The next day, however, brought an unprecedented maelstrom that knocked the entire world sideways. The virus spread rapidly and a worldwide lockdown was announced. What started as 'janta curfew'—a lockdown for a day—got extended for twenty-one days. That is when everyone understood the severity of the situation. There was a mad rush to stock up on groceries and other necessities. There were arrests across the country for violating the lockdown rules such as venturing out when there was no emergency, opening businesses and even violating home quarantine.

Initially, we thought it would pass quickly and things would get back to normal in a few days. However, when more and more people were affected every day, we were told not to step outside. Jasmine got an official email declaring that her office would be shut and the employees were provided with IT connectivity and access to enable them to work from home. I had a few book events to attend, but they were cancelled as well. I was almost done writing the book I was working on, but had no idea when the publishers would be able to release it.

Neerav was the only one who seemed happy that his work had come to a halt; it was a mini, twenty-one-day vacation for him.

Karan was in a similar situation but was far from pleased because Shruti was stuck in Pune, and he worried about her just as she worried about him. If he had known their lives would come to a standstill, he would've tagged along with her to Pune. All they could do was make video calls. They had no choice but to continue in a long-distance relationship. Shruti was miserable to be away from Karan.

They were on a video call when she said, 'Things are only getting worse day by day. I hope I get to return before this lockdown ends. But I don't know how. Travelling in this pandemic is out of the question as only emergency vehicles are allowed to pass.'

'We've no option but to wait for twenty-one days. I hope the situation gets better. There are rumours on WhatsApp that this twenty-one-day period is just eyewash by the government so that people don't go into a blind panic; they say it will probably get extended a lot longer. I don't know how true that is, but I sincerely hope that things get back to normal very soon,' said Karan.

'How's everyone at home? Don't let Aai and Papa go out anywhere. And you, also, please use a mask and sanitizers.'

'We're fine here. You're always surrounded by people there; you're the one who needs to be more careful. I hope we can be together soon. Love you.'

'Love you too.'

No one was prepared for the pandemic or had ever experienced such a calamity before. Whenever the medical staff, in PPE kits, arrived in ambulances to quarantine people, people were petrified. The authorities did their best to allay anxieties, but fear made people do weird things. While a lot of people in poor countries struggled to make ends meet on a daily basis, some turned into vaccine experts and yet others provided entertainment with slogans of 'go, Corona, go', hoping to end the pandemic. But nothing helped and the situation across the board in India only worsened.

On the other hand, Neerav had very different problems in his life and called to say, 'Bro, my health is deteriorating as I see my stock of rum and whiskey dwindling. If the lockdown is extended any further, I'm screwed. How do we replenish our stocks?'

'Don't worry. Come down to my place, I have some good stock for you,' I told him, checking my bar.

'That would be great. It's been a while since we met. Are you done writing the book?'

'Yeah, almost.' I was still at my laptop, writing the last chapter.

'Okay. Are you sure no one will object? Because in my area, they're not allowing outsiders.'

'That I'll manage. You just check to see whether the cops are allowing personal vehicles on the road.'

'They're just doing random checks. It should be fine. Anyway, I believe *karm nahi, kaand karo*. I'll come by in a few hours.' Like me, Neerav thrived in the tension of the situation.

It had been more than a couple of weeks since the lockdown had been imposed and everyone was talking about COVID-19—on news channels, the Internet and social media. There weren't enough rooms or beds in hospitals and therefore, special wards and quarantine facilities had been set up.

It was depressing and more so for us because the building opposite ours had been converted into a quarantine centre, and seeing ambulances every hour with patients, including kids, was disturbing to say the least. I couldn't take it any more and temporarily locked the door leading out into the balcony to avoid the negative vibes.

Just then, Jasmine came to me and said, 'I've received an email from my office saying that they'll be docking our salaries. The future of the project that I'm working on also looks bleak.' She was almost in tears, not knowing how to cope with it.

'Don't worry, everything will be fine,' I comforted her with a hug.

However, only she knew the true extent of the mayhem in her head. She did calm down for a while, until she was suddenly beset by more depressing thoughts. 'How are we supposed to manage if this continues? Your work has come to a halt. Outdoor events have stopped and the television project, which you were working on, also looks doubtful at this stage, especially with the ongoing situation. Book stores are closed, online deliveries have stopped,' she summarized the universal predicament at one go. 'All this is just making me nervous.'

'I understand. But I do think that you're overthinking it. I still feel it won't spread in India to the extent it has in Italy, China and other countries. The lockdown will ease up after April. We have enough savings and there's nothing to worry about. Think about the predicament of those who are surviving on daily wages and what they must be going through. Compared to them, we're in a much better position.'

My monologue didn't relieve her of her anxiety, and the negative thoughts continued to fester in her mind.

'What if I lose my job and the situation doesn't improve for a couple of months or more?'

'Why are you thinking so negatively? The entire world is in the same boat, not just us. We'll find a way. You trust me, right?'

'Of course, I do. But I don't know what's happening to me. I'm tense for many reasons. My parents are alone in Delhi, Bhai is in the US. What if something happens to them? I'll not even be able to travel. When Shruti isn't able to come from Pune, Delhi is out of the question.'

That was when the coin dropped, and I realized exactly what it was that was bothering her. Anyway, there was nothing I could do about it. It was a time of great adversity and if you were far away from your parents, you obviously worried about their health and feared losing them. Her family was her strength, and it was the first time that, despite wanting to meet them, she couldn't. Probably the only positive thing about the lockdown and virus was that it brought families closer than ever before and made us understand the true value of relationships.

* * *

Everybody hoped that things would go to normal soon, but it seemed more and more like this was the new normal. Zoom meetings, ordering everything online, wearing masks, using sanitizers, home parties and so on had become part of life. However, instead of living in fear, we decided to live with faith, believing everything would fall into place soon.

However, destiny had other plans.

The lockdown was further extended until 5 May. The number of cases in India had crossed four digits. The plight of migrants worsened, and even people like us now wondered when this would end. There were a few relaxations for daily essential stores, but everything else stayed shut. I called my publishers to find out what could be done, but they had no answer, and all I could do was look at the online statistics of COVID-19 cases. One thing was for sure, the pandemic made us appreciate the little things in life, things that we always took for granted—be it going into the open for some fresh air or simply hanging out with friends. Karan's work had resumed on a work-from-home basis and although he showed complete dedication, his heart wasn't in it. He had asked all the local authorities he knew if there was a way that Shruti could come back, but the city borders were closed, and they had to wait for them to open.

One day, after dinner, Shruti called Karan.

'Guess what I made today,' she said.

The excitement in her voice was palpable. 'Pav bhaji?'

'No.'

'Halwa?' he guessed again.

'No ... I tried butter garlic prawns for the first time, and they were so yummy.' She sent him a photograph and told him how everyone had been licking their fingers. 'I'm sure you would have loved it. For the first time, I, myself, was impressed by my cooking.'

'Wow, I think this lockdown will turn you into a strong contender in *MasterChef*,' Karan teased. 'How unlucky I am. Everyone is eating the food cooked by my wife, but me. Now, when you return, you'll have to again make all the dishes that I am missing out on.'

'For sure, my darling hubby. But why haven't you accepted my ludo request yet? Are you afraid you'll lose again?' she pouted.

'Fuck that, I'm not playing. That game is rigged, I'm sure of it now,' said Karan.

'You're such a spoilsport. Just because you lose, does it automatically mean that the game is rigged?'

'Obviously, it is. You keep getting six, six and five every time you roll the dice. Even when only one of my tokens is out and I need one, I don't get it and you win the game. It's deeply annoying, it is! I'm not playing.'

Shruti laughed. 'That's because after marriage, wives are meant to win—be it in an argument or in a game.'

'Funny. Anyway, I have to clean my room right now.'

'Just throwing your trash outside the room doesn't count as cleaning the room,' Shruti mocked him.

'Oh really? Wait, let me show rather than tell.' Karan switched the camera and showed her the vacuum cleaner in the room, along with a broom.

'That's impressive. Learn some more skills so that my work becomes easier when I come home.'

Karan switched back to the front camera but didn't react. He just made comical faces at her, telling her not to underestimate him.

Shruti added, 'But why are you cleaning the room right now?'

'Because you aren't here and I have nothing to do,' Karan replied.

'And what if I were there? What would you have done?'

'You want to know?' Karan winked lasciviously.

'Yes,' Shruti groaned.

'I would've first kissed you and then pushed you on to the bed. Would you like that?' Karan's excitement and desire were waging a war.

'Keep talking . . .' she adjusted herself on the bed and tried to control her breathing. She switched the video call to audio, and Karan immediately protested.

'Why? I want to see you.'

'No . . . I feel shy, and I just want to hear your voice right now. Please continue.'

Karan didn't want to miss the moment and although slightly disappointed, he continued, 'Now, take off your top.'

The authority in his voice had her hands reaching for the buttons of her top. The cool air touched her bare skin.

'Is it off?' he asked.

'Yes.'

Settling back on the soft cushions, he placed the phone close to his head and put it on speaker. He wanted it so bad. He heard Shruti say,

'Now what?'

'You sound very turned on, Shruti. Now, play with yourself,' Karan's breathing was harsh, his whispers rougher.

'God,' Shruti moaned.

'Does that feel good, baby?'

'Yes,' Shruti bit her lip in pleasure.

It struck her that this might be her only chance to feel this way. As soon as they were back together, this wouldn't be possible. The realization intensified her need and made her desperate. Every word Karan spoke was a spear of pleasure to her throbbing desire. She shut her eyes. Just then, he heard a knock at the door.

'Fucking hell . . . I am screwed!' Karan muttered and got up to straighten his clothes.

'Why? What happened?' Shruti asked.

'Nothing . . . Dad's here. I'll talk to you later. I'm so sorry. We will finish what we began.'

'Love you, baby,' Shruti said before disconnecting the call, slightly disappointed.

Karan opened the door, 'Do you need anything, Papa?' He was scared his dad had heard whatever was going on inside the room.

'What were you doing?' his father asked.

Fuck, I think he heard my moans. What should I say now?

'Nothing, why, what happened?' Karan stammered in fear.

'I meant, are you working right now or are you free to talk?' he asked, peeping into his room to see if the laptop was on.

Karan sighed in relief. 'Yes, I'm free. Tell me.'

'Actually . . . I had a word with one of my friends who knows some of the local authorities well, who can arrange for an e-pass for Shruti to come back to Mumbai. Ask her if she's okay with that.'

Karan's heart soared in joy. He would be able to meet Shruti at long last and after so long. He missed doing simple things with her, like holding hands, sharing a meal or watching movies, and had waited patiently and eagerly to relive those moments again. Unwilling to get his hopes up, he asked whether that was really possible. His dad nodded in affirmation. Karan immediately conveyed the astounding news to Shruti. She was thrilled to bits.

'Whatever we stopped midway, let's finish soon, in real life,' she texted him before falling asleep.

'I'm desperately waiting for some real action,' Karan replied. Indeed, together, they made life look beautiful.

Chapter 5

Karan and Shruti had been impatiently counting the hours until they could be together again. Shruti was able to get back home along with her parents without any hassles. She first dropped them home and then made her way to Karan; her heart racing, her desperation increasing with every minute.

She shed happy tears to be back home where everyone loved and missed her. More than the pain of separation, the happiness of reuniting again was visible in their eyes. Touching someone you love after a long separation feels like that first refreshing glass of cold water when you've been dehydrated or the moment you resurface to breathe after swimming underwater for too long. It feels like survival. The way they picked up the threads from where they had left off was like they had never been separated and no time had passed at all. That moment was proof of their invincible connection with each other and nothing could have severed it.

'Feels so good that you are back home and safe. I was worried while you were on the way back. Did they allow you in easily?' Karan's mother asked her.

'They did check the e-pass and inquired the reason for travelling, but didn't create a ruckus because, as Papa had mentioned, we made him talk to the authority who had given us the e-pass.'

'Now, you relax. You did take all precautions on the way, right?'

'Yes, Aai, don't worry.' Shruti took the glass of water that her mother-in-law had brought for her.

'God knows when all this will end. We are fed up with wearing masks every time we go down or someone knocks on the door.'

Shruti just smiled. She knew it wasn't easy, but it was the only way to stay safe. Karan's dad, who had been hovering around them, said, 'Karan told us that you cooked some amazing dishes in Pune. You must make them for us also in the coming days.'

'Sure, Papa.'

Karan stood by, listening to them, impatiently waiting for their pleasantries to be done so he could get Shruti all to himself in the privacy of their room.

He didn't have to wait long. As soon as the door closed behind them, Shruti went over to the window by the bed. She heard him walk up behind her and sensed him draw closer.

Karan stopped her from turning, 'Don't. I just want to feel you.'

Her heart began to pound. She stood there, feeling desire drip from her heart, down towards her inner thighs. Karan's fingers lightly touched her neck as he gently brushed aside her hair, and it gave her goosebumps. His hands went from the sides of her head down to her neck, to her shoulders and then slid down. He held her hands gently, but firmly, and paused. She felt safe and said nothing. She had already closed her eyes, feeling his every touch; her breathing had turned heavy, and the soft moans from her mouth drove Karan to ecstasy. He kissed her shoulder and ran his lips towards her ear. She tilted her head and felt his warm breath over her skin as he bit her gently. She craved more. He turned her towards him, and they stood facing each other. Karan looked deep into Shruti's eyes and smiled.

'I love you,' he said.

'I love you more than you love me. Let's finish where we left off,' Shruti whispered, moving closer and unbuttoning his shirt.

But he stopped her and said, 'Not so fast . . . you've made me wait for so long . . . I've been desperate for this moment.'

His hands grabbed her left hand and held her palm against his heart. His eyes exuded love, desire, care and respect. She smiled and he released her hand and gently guided her face closer until her head rested on his chest. He wrapped his other arm around her, and they both hoped never to be away from each other again. Karan took a step back and gazed at her, from head to toe, with slow deliberation. The air between them almost crackled.

She yearned to move in and close the gap between them again but remained where she was as his eyes lingered on her lips for a moment before lifting his gaze to meet her eyes. He pushed her on to the bed and climbed on her. Soothed by his embrace, she remained still and relaxed, melting into him. She hadn't expected such intensity, although she ought to have. That night had the power to change her world. It was in that moment that she realized she was his and he was hers. They wished to prolong that moment forever, just feeling their bodies against each other.

As soon as they were done, Shruti curled herself against his chest and said, 'I missed you.' She punched his chest lightly, like it was his fault that they had been apart.

'I missed you too,' Karan said. 'I feel like . . .'

'What?' she asked. 'How do you feel? Tell me.'

Karan smiled at her curiosity.

'Like you were never far away. Like you were always here beside me. Like nothing could separate us . . . ever.'

'Really?' She blushed and looked into his eyes. 'But what if someone more beautiful than me were to come into your life?'

Karan didn't expect that from her and drew back to demand, 'Why do you ask this?'

Shruti played with his fingers. Her voice was choked slightly as she said, 'Nothing . . . being away from you, I realized that now my life revolves around you, and I can't live without you. I never thought that I would fall in love so deeply, but the distance made me love you even more. Never leave me. Ever.'

Karan kissed her forehead and said, 'Why would I leave my beautiful wife for someone else? I love you.'

As the two loving souls were reunited, they felt their hearts beating for each other. Some relationships are just meant to happen, and you don't need a reason. Karan and Shruti had fallen in love after getting married, and when they looked back, it seemed destiny and the cosmos had conspired to bring them together.

* * *

'So, what's the story of your next book then?' Neerav asked me.

Now that Shruti was back, the group had convened at my home as we hadn't been together after our Goa trip.

'It's about a girl giving herself a second chance to fall in love. It's about loving oneself and not being too hard on oneself when one fails in love. Basically, it's the story of her arranged marriage and how she overcomes her fear of failure in relationships.'

'Arranged marriage? Are you writing Karan's story from Shruti's point of view with some spice in it?'

I laughed when both Karan and Shruti looked at me, shocked. 'Why are you taking Neerav so seriously? You know how he is. There's no reason to worry. It's not your story.'

'You could've at least played along for a while,' Neerav was crestfallen to have lost a golden opportunity to make fun of the newlyweds again. 'Anyway, how are you coping with all this? I mean, your book is almost done but you don't know when it will release as the bookstores are still closed.'

'Not easy, for sure. Everything has gone for a toss, but there's nothing we can do at present.' I didn't go into the details because, lately, the more I thought about it, the more the fear which kept me awake at night.

Karan looked at the watch and announced, all of a sudden, 'It's 7 p.m., Modiji is supposed to be live. Switch on the television. Let's hear what he has to say.'

'Trust me, whenever he's live on TV these days, I get the heebie-jeebies wondering which bomb he's going to drop this time.'

Shruti grinned, 'I totally agree.'

When Jasmine switched on the news channel, the headlines were already scrolling on the ticker tape. The lockdown had been extended until 17 May. I felt even more frustrated. Despite telling Jasmine not to overthink things, I had started doing exactly the same thing over the last few days, and the extension of the lockdown only exacerbated my worry. Although I pretended to be fine and stayed calm on the outside, a storm of negative thoughts was brewing inside me, thinking about the uncertainty ahead and alternative ways out.

When Karan began complaining about how boring it was to work from home, I couldn't control myself, 'Bhai, at least you have work and are getting paid for it. Respect that. Think about all those who have no work and are forced to sit idle at home. Think about small businesses that are completely shut. Think about people like me, whose work has come to a complete halt. And despite being ready to work for more hours than you do, we've no option but to just wait until the lockdown is lifted. You'll probably never know that kind of insecurity and keep talking shit.'

It was only after I had vented my spleen that I felt I had gone too far by attacking him personally.

However, he retaliated with something even worse, 'Did I ever talk about all the royalties that you got all these years, that was way more than what we were getting paid? Do we get the celebrity status that you get? Don't talk nonsense! You think we have it easy and you're the only one suffering?' He had raised his voice by now.

I didn't hold back either, 'Where the fuck did "celebrity status" come from? And when the fuck did I say that it's easy for you? You're behaving like an immature dickhead!'

'Yeah, and I've seen your maturity when you went to massage parlours to fuck and do whatnot.' Karan stood up. It all happened so quickly that no one could gauge what was right and what was wrong. Perhaps nothing was wrong, but in the heat of the moment, neither he nor I gave way.

Things had already spiralled out of control by the time Jasmine interrupted and shouted, 'Will you both stop? What's wrong with you? Have you both completely lost it?'

Neerav tugged worriedly at Karan's sleeve, 'Do you even realize what you're saying? You're crossing the line.'

'Why don't you say the same to your best friend? Isn't he crossing all the limits? Anyway, I'm done with this.'

Shruti tried to placate Karan, but he impatiently took her hand and walked out of the house in a monumental huff. Silent glances were exchanged between Neerav, Jasmine and me before he walked out, but no one said a word or tried to stop him.

It felt terrible, but ego and why-the-fuck-should-I-make-the-first-move came between us. It wasn't like we hadn't had arguments before, but we had never gone this far, ever. For days, we didn't talk to each other. There were times when Neerav attempted to reconcile us, but both Karan and I were too stubborn and intractable.

Neerav even said, 'Time will pass and both of you may come to regret what you said.'

Jasmine also did her best to make me see sense, to shelve my stubborn pride and end this pointless feuding with a good friend. It wasn't like I didn't want to make up, but there was a lot on my mind. I tried not to let the lockdown situation get me down emotionally, but with each passing day, it was getting tougher for en number of reasons. The lockdown was extended to June, and every negative thought, about paying for EMIs, bills and all the other household essentials, relentlessly gnawed at my mind. I didn't discuss these issues even with Jasmine, as I didn't want to worry her unnecessarily. It was difficult to convey this to anyone and only I knew the extent of my mental turmoil.

It's said that every storm eventually runs out of rain, but this downpour seemed endless. Before I could discuss my state of mind with Jasmine, she gave me some news that kept me from revealing my anxieties to her.

'I've been told that my project will be wrapping up soon. Remember, I told you that I had a strong feeling that this would happen. They're saying as the company isn't getting new projects in this uncertain climate, both politically and financially, they will . . .' she trailed off, looking devastated.

I thought for a while and then said, 'I think it's better that you hand in your resignation. I always told you that this job is taking a toll on your health, with more than four hours of commute time every day, from our place to Nariman Point. I think it's time you moved on. I'm sure you'll find better options in the future.'

I didn't let her see that I was equally downcast by the news. None of this was her fault anyway. These were tough times, and if I had revealed my despair, she would've been shattered. Upon seeing my unswerving support and understanding, she broke down sobbing like a child in my arms, feeling utterly helpless in the face of such setbacks. I dried her tears and pampered her. She eventually pulled herself together and sniffled, 'But the entire burden will be on you then, and you know I don't like that. I don't want to be a burden to you, I want to be your strength.'

'You'll always be my strength, Jasmine. You could never be a burden. Never think like that. I love you.'

A watery smile appeared on her face. The stillness of the atmosphere spoke volumes, and I knew just how much she was hurting. She was feeling too low to express anything, nevertheless she did as she was told, albeit with a heavy heart.

We did whatever we could, but within a week I got a call from the production house and the partner with whom I was working on a script for a television show, 'We did like the script you sent, it's fresh and new, but unfortunately, Aditya, we won't be able to take it forward as the channel is currently putting new projects on hold. Shooting has stopped, and with no idea when it would resume, they don't want to commit to anything new for now. Maybe, until then, we just keep improvising on the script and then pitch it to some other channel.'

That was just their subtle way of saying, 'fuck off, we don't need any scripts right now'. I knew this because it wasn't my first rejection; it was heartbreaking nevertheless, because we had worked together on the script for almost half a year and had almost completed it. The production house was equally taken aback because they too had expected things to be finalized in the meeting. They did assure me that the script would find a place on some channel, but these were mere platitudes that didn't make me feel any better. I kept these things to myself and didn't tell Jasmine. Unfortunately, the more I kept things bottled up, the further it pushed me to the edge of the precipice. To make matters worse, I had developed a severe writer's block and sat staring at a blank page on the laptop screen all day without writing a word.

Am I finished? Will I never find the inspiration to write again? I wondered. It wasn't the rejection, for sure—I was strong enough to handle those, but my mind was preoccupied with the innumerable insecurities that suddenly loomed large. Every second of every day, I thought of putting an end to it all. But couldn't. I had everything going for me until, out of nowhere, I felt someone or something nudging me off that cliff, and I was terrified of what waited below; with each passing day, my will to fight problems and overcome them diminished.

My heart said that I should share what I was going through with someone, but my brain prevented me from doing so. It drove me insane, to a point where I resorted to alcohol and meaningless music to distract myself from my self-destructive thoughts. I felt good only as long as I was high. Once I became sober, I again fell prey to the demons that gnawed at my very soul.

Every day, I forced myself to crawl out of bed and live another day that consisted of the same fucking monotonous routine where I scrolled through social media in an attempt to escape the loneliness in my mind; however, seeing people flaunting their lockdown pictures only depressed me further. I tried doing the same and uploaded happy, upbeat pictures, thinking that that would help; but, at the end of the day, nothing mattered.

I kept asking myself why I couldn't be like them for a change. This was not the person I used to be. Could it be possible that they were also pretending, like me? I had no fucking idea. I was emotionally empty and mourned the happiness that I had lost. My mind was preoccupied with the events which had triggered this state of mind, and I pondered on the source of my misery. I felt like I was letting everyone down but was clueless about why this was happening to me. The negativity in the air, with so many deaths and so many people losing their livelihoods, made me feel even more miserable. I was literally living a dual life. One on the outside, where I made everyone believe there was nothing wrong with me; and another on the inside, where I felt there was nothing going right. But still, it reflected in my behaviour and one evening, when I was high on alcohol, a small argument with Jasmine escalated into something brutal.

'What have I said to make you fly off the handle like this? I only asked you to keep your things in their place so that the room looks tidy. Is that such a big deal?' Jasmine shouted from the bedroom.

Initially, I didn't react and just sat around on the recliner sofa in the living room, waiting for the storm to blow over. However, when she went into a loop, repeating the same thing over and over again, I got up and went into the bedroom.

'But I don't want to. I like my room when it's messy, when my stuff is all over the place. Is that such a big deal? This is my house, and I can do whatever I want to do. I'm paying the loans and bills, and managing everything, so let me do what I want to do. Don't teach me what's right and wrong.'

And then, Jasmine blew her stack, 'Oh wow, so you're singing a different tune now, aren't you? Weren't you the one who advised me to take a step back? Now you're hinting that I'm a parasite living off you.'

'Oh man, this is crazy!' I threw my hands up in disgust, 'Look, I'm already going through a lot, and I don't want to hear these nonsensical lectures. It would be better if you thought about our future rather than keeping this house fucking clean.'

'Fine, I'll book tickets to Delhi tomorrow, then you live in your own house . . . alone.' She opened her laptop and ignored me.

'Do whatever you want.' I walked out before she could slam the bedroom door on my face. She eventually did slam the door.

It was only the next day that the enormity of what I had done dawned on me. I immediately tried to patch things up, but she was still extremely upset. Throughout that day, I received more than a few parcels of online orders without showing any irritation and faking excitement; I even clicked a lot of photographs and made reels for her that she was supposed to make for product endorsement, with all the enthusiasm I could muster. That eventually mellowed her down. That's how the relationship changes after years of marriage; from flowers and bouquets to doing these little things to mend fights. But what was disheartening was the realization that I was losing myself day by day and turning into a person I wasn't. I had to find a way out of this labyrinth before it was too late.

Chapter 6

Have you ever said something in anger just to inflict pain, but regretted it later? And thought about how you could've responded in a number of different ways to avoid the fight? It had been days, but neither Karan nor I had reached out to each other. There were times I picked up the phone to call him or text him when I saw him online on WhatsApp, but didn't, thinking he didn't care. Karan, too, felt the same, which Neerav conveyed to me several times. But still, no words were exchanged until one Sunday, when I eventually called him. He didn't answer my call, and after that I didn't try again, thinking he wasn't ready to reconcile.

Karan did see the missed call later, but Shruti wasn't well, and he was worried about her. He decided to call me back later as she had been ill for the past couple of days, her symptoms ranging from fever to loss of appetite. Even at this point in time, she lay curled up in bed, shivering.

'I hope you're feeling somewhat better,' said Karan as he helped her sit up. He had prepared her favourite chicken soup just so that she could eat something nutritious. She had skipped both lunch and dinner that day. Karan had convinced her to have some of the soup and drink a cup of tea. Shruti took one spoonful of the soup and gagged. It was godawful. She wondered whether Karan had used stale chicken or some other ingredient that was way too pungent.

'Did you use the fresh chicken that was in the fridge?'

'Yes, my love. Why?' He had carefully measured out all the ingredients and had tasted the soup himself. It was delicious. 'It's absolutely fine,' he defended his culinary experiment. He felt that she was simply making lame excuses to starve herself. 'What's wrong? Don't make flimsy excuses for not eating it.'

'It tastes horrible,' she shuddered. 'I'll have the tea, please.'

Karan gave her the green tea which he had brought along with the soup. She felt queasy. She took a tentative sip and then threw up. Karan helped change her clothes and cleaned up the vomit. He covered her in a blanket and said, worriedly, 'We need to go to the doctor. We can't just sit around, waiting for you to get better.' Karan checked her temperature. She was still feverish.

'I'll be fine. I don't want to go to the hospital during COVID,' Shruti protested in a weak voice.

'No problem. I'll ask the family doctor to pay us a home visit tomorrow.' Karan didn't want to take any risks. At first, he had assumed she had caught the virus and had isolated her, but her test results were negative. He still didn't want to risk it and had telephoned the doctor and asked him to visit them the following day. By the time he finished the call, Shruti was already fast asleep. He sat beside her and picked up his mobile from the bedside table.

Should I call Aditya? But it's already so late, and I don't want to disturb him when he's asleep; it will be better if I call him tomorrow. But what should I say after all that has happened? Did he really call to apologize or only because Neerav told him to do so?

He slept a troubled sleep, mulling over these thoughts.

Shruti hadn't yet told her mother she was ill. She hadn't wanted to unnecessarily worry her parents and also, she wanted to wait for the COVID-test result. The next morning, when Shruti woke up, she telephoned her mother and told her she was unwell.

To Shruti's amazement, her mother got all excited at this disclosure, 'That's great news!'

Shruti couldn't understand what she was on about and asked her mother in a strained voice, 'I'm feeling terrible here and that's good news for you?'

'How foolish you are. Nothing has happened to you. Go and buy yourself a home-pregnancy-test kit and take care of yourself. You're pregnant!'

'What are you—' before Shruti could complete her sentence, her mother had hung up to share the good news with her dad.

It was only then she realized she had missed her cycle last month. Earlier, she thought it was because of the stress, but maybe her mother was right. She didn't quite know how to react. But before she could fully assimilate her mother's diagnosis, Karan came in with breakfast.

'Okay. You look a lot better today. Got some sleep?'

Shruti nodded, still consumed by the thought of being pregnant. She didn't reveal the possibility to Karan and merely said, 'I hate colds and fevers. They sap all your energy, and it feels pathetic to lie about in bed all day.'

Karan placed the breakfast on the bedside table and said cheerfully, 'Don't worry. The doctor will be here at any moment. I'm going to buy the groceries that Aai had listed last night. If you need anything—anything at all—do tell Aai and Papa.'

Shruti assured him that she would eat the breakfast. As soon as Karan left, she lay back on the bed, deeply cogitating. She felt chills go down her spine. They hadn't planned for this, and although she was happy, she didn't know how Karan would react if it turned out to be true.

A little later, Karan came in along with the doctor, having run into him downstairs near the gate of their colony. Shruti told the doctor about the nausea she had had for the past few days. He ran a quick, general check-up and handed over a prescription to Karan.

Karan's mother, who was hovering anxiously at the door, asked the doctor in a tense voice, 'Is everything all right, doctor? Her COVID test was negative. There's nothing to be worried about, right?'

'She's absolutely fine,' the doctor replied with a smile, and looking at Shruti, asked, 'When was the last time you had your period?'

Shruti hadn't expected him to ask that personal question so bluntly and in front of everyone. Karan's father was standing there too, and she felt deeply embarrassed. Both Karan and Shruti looked at each other; Karan, unaware of where this line of questioning was leading, was obviously more shocked than she was.

'I missed it last month and this month as well,' Shruti slowly realized that her mother's diagnosis might have been spot on.

A slight smile appeared on Karan and his parents' faces. They all looked at the doctor, anticipating what was coming their way.

He snapped shut his bag and said, 'She still has a fever. I've prescribed the medicines that will make her feel better, and some vitamin tablets too, so that she will feel energetic. However, I think she needs to take a pregnancy test—either at home or at the lab—because I think she's expecting.'

Karan's parents escorted the doctor out. The minute they were alone in their bedroom, Karan rushed to Shruti's side.

'Shruti . . .' he held her hands and kissed her. 'Which test do you prefer?'

Her heartbeat accelerated suddenly. 'I'll do it at home. No labs, please. I'm scared, Karan.'

'Why?' he held her close.

'Are you ready for this? It's a big decision,' she asked nervously.

'Of course, I am. We're in this together.' His response relieved Shruti a bit and she snuggled into his arms.

Later, when Shruti emerged from the bathroom after running the test, Karan's eyes, which had been glued to the bathroom door, were unblinkingly on her, trying to predict the result by the expression on her face. He saw her face shining, lit up with the most adorable smile he had even ever seen. It melted his heart once again.

'We're expecting, Karan . . . we're pregnant!' she announced.

Karan would never forget that moment, knowing their lives were about to change forever; she protectively cradled her belly and smiled for hours. Mixed in with all the joy, excitement and anticipation, was uncertainty, fear and questions like 'how the fuck are we going to do this?' But that's always the way it was and will be.

* * *

The same evening, Neerav called to tell me that Karan was soon going to be a father. I couldn't believe my ears and was overjoyed to hear that one of my best friends was about to enter a new phase in his life. But the very next moment, I remembered that I was not on talking terms with him and I felt terrible thinking about how our friendship had turned sour.

Neerav sensed my ambivalence and said, 'I'm going to meet him now. I feel you should come along. This isn't the time to hold grudges. He'll definitely welcome you with open arms and let bygones be bygones. You should let go of your stupid pride, Bhai!'

My impulse was to hang up immediately and go and hug Karan, forgiving and forgetting everything, but something held me back. 'I haven't spoken to him all this while . . . do you think he's still upset over our fall out?'

'You're a dumbass. He'll be upset if you don't come along. Trust me.' Neerav was preaching to the choir, because I was already sold on the idea of burying the hatchet and to kiss and make up with Karan.

When I told Jasmine about Karan and Shruti, she was thrilled and without a moment's hesitation, asked if we could go over to see them. There was no way I could have denied going when it was such a big moment in Karan's life. All the shared memories at the various phases of our lives flashed before my eyes. He had been there whenever I needed him, during the times I was unsure about my writing. In every success and every failure, he stood by me. And I was speechless thinking how far we had come in this journey of friendship.

All through the drive to his home, I kept thinking about the best way to apologize to him and what I should say. The moment we reached his place, words failed me. Karan had tears in his eyes to see me, along with Neerav and Jasmine.

'I knew you would come,' he said.

My eyes were moist for two reasons. The first was obvious, he was entering parenthood; and second, because it felt like nothing had changed between us.

'Why wouldn't I? After all, I love you and no matter what, I'll always be there. Congratulations to both of you,' I said as he embraced me and broke down in my arms.

'There were so many times when I thought I should call you,' wept Karan, 'but then I wondered why you weren't calling me. I felt that I had perhaps crossed a line and ruined everything. Yesterday, when you called, that was when I knew that you must be feeling the same; and that, after finding out the good news, you would come.' He paused and then grinned. 'I would've killed you if you hadn't come today.'

'Now chill and enjoy the moment. You are going to be a father,' I said bracingly.

Jasmine and Shruti, too, were emotional and hugged each other. Seeing Karan and me, Neerav laughed, 'That's so typical of you guys: you said something to him, he said something to you, and things just boiled over. One of you could've taken the other's remark with a pinch of salt, but nooooo . . . and then you do all this soppy soap opera stuff now. I wonder what Shruti must think of us.' He laughed.

Neerav wasn't far wrong. We never questioned whether our friendship could withstand the friendly fire. Not many friends can do what we do—speak our mind frankly without faking a smile and pretending that everything is just hunky dory. The truth is, real friendships, which last for years and decades, which span the coming and going of lovers and jobs and difficult times, as well as joyous ones, are forged in the fire of arguments and disagreements. Such friendships only grow stronger and last eternally.

* * *

'The sonography report has come,' Karan announced in a tense voice. He had gone to collect the reports from the gynaecologist whom their family doctor had recommended. Hearing these words, Shruti, and even his parents, looked nervous.

What could it be? Is my baby okay? No . . . no . . . nothing could have happened to him, thought Shruti, caressing her stomach, trying to feel the presence of the life evolving in her.

'Is everything all right? Why do you sound so low?' Shruti whispered in fear.

Karan's mother was the most anxious and couldn't handle the needless suspense that Karan was creating. 'The baby is okay, right? What's the issue?' she demanded stridently.

Before any more drama could ensue, Karan revealed that he had just been kidding. 'The baby and Shruti are both in good condition. I was just playing the fool.'

Shruti scowled at him. She had been scared shitless for a moment.

Karan's mother, infuriated with his silliness, scolded him roundly, 'This isn't funny. You shouldn't do such things and make her anxious at this time. What would you have done if the sudden shock had created complications?'

Karan apologized and sat down beside Shruti. He held her hand and said, 'But the doctor has asked us to visit her in the clinic tomorrow. Perhaps it's for a routine check-up or for some instructions that she wants to give us.'

The next day, when Shruti was getting ready, she looked at her wardrobe and wondered how on earth she was going to squeeze into these clothes after a few months.

'Karan, will I have to change my entire wardrobe in the coming days?' she asked as she rummaged through her closet for the loose clothes that the doctor had prescribed.

'Why do you say that? You have so many clothes. I don't understand why girls think they have nothing to wear despite taking half of their husband's wardrobe space,' Karan replied, peering into her closet.

'Idiot. I won't fit into more than half of these in a few months,' she said. That triggered a swarm of doubts in her mind, and she added, 'Do you think I'll be able to handle it all? I mean, I'll be able to walk properly, right, even when I'm as big as a house?'

Karan was gazing at her, laughing at her crazy concerns. Shruti punched his chest for not taking her seriously. 'Will you stop laughing? I'm really worried.'

'Stop worrying so much.' Karan held her face affectionately with both his hands.

'But only you can answer me and that's why I'm asking you.' Shruti looked up at him impishly.

'How will I know?'

'Because you can tell me if you feel uncomfortable when you walk.' She covered her mouth to control her laughter.

'No,' replied Karan spontaneously, before understanding the full import of her cheeky insinuation.

His expression changed suddenly, his eyebrows disappearing into his hairline in disbelief. Shruti was laughing hard, her head thrown back, thoroughly enjoying his outrage.

'Are you making fun of me? I don't have a beer belly. You can check it yourself.'

He lifted his shirt to prove his point, but eventually, they both started to giggle at their silly discussion. They were enjoying this phase and their new journey towards parenthood. Not every day was easy; sometimes it was emotionally draining for both parents-to-be, but sometimes it was the best feeling ever. And every second was worth it.

He remembered what his dad had said when the good news had been disclosed to him, 'Make Shruti feel like she is a queen, because she is creating a life. Make her smile every damn day because her view of her own self will change. She'll think that the weight gain is making her less beautiful, but you should often convey the reality to her that she looks more beautiful than ever. I know, because I have gone through it all, and that's the best advice I can give you.'

Karan had tears of joy when his dad told him to enjoy the experience.

Shruti often got emotional and fatigued with all the stress, with her body aches and having to use the bathroom several times a day; there were times she couldn't explain the melancholy, but Karan stood by her like a pillar of strength and made her feel that it was okay to cry or get upset and he made her feel like she was the most beautiful woman on earth.

When they got to the hospital, the doctor checked Shruti's blood pressure and said, 'I would recommend that you avoid any food that is high in glucose.'

Shruti sat silently as Karan looked seriously at the doctor. 'What type of food would be suitable for her?' he asked curiously.

'What do you eat?' the doctor directed the question at Shruti.

'My head, for sure,' Karan mocked her to lighten the mood. The doctor couldn't help smiling. Shruti asked the doctor to ignore him and continue.

'Shruti, you should eat protein-rich food, more water and vegetables. I don't think I need to say that no alcohol or even caffeine. And stop getting stressed out. Pregnant women are prone to high blood pressure.'

'Alcohol I can do without, but caffeine?' Shruti always had a cup of coffee in the morning and that was something she couldn't live without. But the doctor strictly forbade it.

Karan, who was enjoying the moment, purposely asked, 'I can have caffeine and alcohol, right?'

'You can do whatever you want. Your work is done,' said the doctor. Karan laughed at Shruti's expression upon hearing that.

'You have a car, right?' the doctor asked and wrote something in her file. 'You shouldn't travel on two-wheelers or autorickshaws. And keep your seat belt loose, always.'

Karan continued pulling Shruti's leg. 'Isn't there some instruction about not fighting with your husband?'

The doctor didn't react this time. However, Shruti smacked him.

As soon as they exited the doctor's clinic, Shruti said dolefully, 'Everything else is fine, but why no coffee?'

'Don't worry, my love, you can have as much of it as you like after a few months,' Karan consoled her, holding her hand.

'How do you know so much?' Shruti questioned, suppressing her smile.

'I've researched it, of course. We're both pregnant. What did you think?' Karan chuckled, making Shruti laugh out loud.

However, it seemed their happiness was meant to be short-lived. Floating on their bubble of optimism, they were blithely unaware of the gathering storm clouds over the horizon which threatened to soak them to the skin and squelch all their plans in the months to come.

A few days later, Karan felt weak and run down and then came down with a high temperature. He immediately isolated himself. His condition didn't improve, and he took a COVID-19 test, hoping against hope that his test result would be negative. Unfortunately, he tested COVID positive. Their whole world seemed to be coming apart at the seams right before their eyes.

Shruti was in shock and the fact that she wasn't allowed to meet him, given her delicate condition, only made her feel worse. Karan's parents comforted her, saying that everything would be okay.

The desolation of isolation was sheer torture for Karan. Nothing made him feel better. *How on earth could this have happened to me? I took all the precautions and was extra careful because Shruti is pregnant. Now what if Shruti, too, turns out to be positive? She's carrying our child. What if something worse happens? How will I survive this catastrophe? I only hope nothing happens to her and my family. I feel terrible right now.*

He felt numb.

Chapter 7

I still wonder how . . . did I get infected when we went to the doctor's clinic in the hospital or when I went to the office? I'm still unable to breathe freely. With every passing moment, it feels like the virus is tightening its stranglehold on me and killing me slowly from the inside. I feel so weak that I can barely get off my bed. Should I tell Shruti and my parents, or will they get needlessly worried? Aai said that sudden shocks aren't good for Shruti. Will she be able to handle it if I tell her that I feel my condition is deteriorating?

As the old adage goes, an idle mind is the devil's workshop. Although Karan's mind, in his weakened state, dwelt on all the worst-case scenarios, he kept his gloomy forebodings to himself.

The onset of the virus had been subtle and had come out of nowhere, with an innocuous tickle in the throat. He had promptly isolated himself so as to not risk the lives of others. The next night, he started feeling worse and developed such a bad headache that he had to cough softly to avoid discomfort. The antibiotics didn't work. Gradually every ounce of energy from his body was depleted, and now, he had even developed a slight breathing problem. He knew it was wrong to keep these symptoms to himself when he ought to have flagged it to his family, but he felt it was bearable and hoped he would soon feel better. He washed his face to camouflage his exhaustion and video-called Shruti.

'Have your test results come? It has been more than twenty-four hours now,' he said in a weary voice.

'Not yet . . . but how are you feeling now? Any better?' Shruti asked; the underlying panic was evident in her tone.

'Slightly,' he lied, but Shruti could see the paleness of his face and his struggle to even speak properly.

'You are lying just so I won't worry, right?'

'No, believe me . . . I'm slightly better than I was yesterday,' Karan lied again. 'Are you or my parents feeling any symptoms?'

'Not yet. We're fine and we want you to get well soon. We need you to be with us, especially me. I can't go through all this alone. You promised to stay with me. So, to honour that promise, you have to recover fast.' Shruti's eyes were moist.

'Don't cry. If you won't be strong, how will I have the strength to overcome this?' Karan comforted her, despite lacking the energy to even hold his phone.

Shruti smiled through her tears, assuring him that she would take care of herself.

Karan felt horrible, being unable to meet any of his family members despite living in the same house.

Although his mother or Shruti left a tray outside his room without fail for every meal, he yearned for their touch, warmth and affection. He had to battle not only the virus but also the demons in his thoughts. Although Shruti and his parents gave him moral support in every possible way, it was only when their test results came back negative that he felt a slight lifting of his spirits. His mother announced it to him from outside his door.

'*Beta*, we've all tested negative, so don't worry about us. And if you feel uneasy at any time, even if it's after midnight, just telephone us or ring the bell. Don't hesitate to tell us anything. We're all with you.'

They had given him a little bell, in case, for some reason, he wasn't able to raise his voice to call for help. Shruti told him she had told Neerav and Jasmine about his condition and they were arranging a bed in the hospital in readiness for the worst-case scenario.

'They've gone mad. I'll be as fit as a fiddle soon, I tell you. I don't need to go to the hospital. Tell them not to overthink it.'

'We, too, hope for the same, touch wood; but they said there's a shortage of beds and we want to be ready in case of an emergency,' replied Shruti.

'What kind of friends have I got?' he complained bitterly. 'On the one hand, they ask me on the phone whether I've read some book or the other or watched some movie on Netflix; and on the other hand, without even telling me, they're trying to book a hospital bed for me. I don't understand what they want.'

Neerav and I kept motivating him and talked about trivial things so that his mood stayed cheerful, but Karan told us that he hadn't responded to even urgent emails from work as he felt too tired to do anything but lie in bed and sleep. However, Neerav's decision to look for a bed in case of emergency proved to be for the best as, within the next few days, Karan's oxygen level suddenly plummeted below 90. He found it extremely difficult to breathe, almost as if someone had placed several bricks on his chest. His parents wasted no time and called an ambulance immediately. He was rushed to a hospital in Navi Mumbai as there was not even a single bed available in Thane.

Shruti was crying uncontrollably and even though Karan's parents were equally shattered, they stood stolidly by Shruti so that her health wasn't affected.

'Aai, please tell them that we can take care of him. We were maintaining social distancing, right? Then why has he been taken to the hospital? He said that day that he doesn't need hospitalization and that he would be fit and fine in a few days,' Shruti sobbed in her mother-in-law's arms.

'Yes, he'll come back after recovering. That's why this was necessary, beta. You also know that he'll get the best possible treatment here, treatment that wasn't possible at home. And don't you want him to recover quickly and return so that you can plan for the baby?'

'But now we won't be able to even see him. At home, at least he was in the same space; and what if he needs me there? Who'll take care of him like I did?' Shruti expressed her grief with a heavy heart.

Karan's father put his hand on her head to comfort her but didn't say a word. He was talking with the hospital authorities and managing the finances so that Karan wouldn't face any problems in the hospital.

When Shruti telephoned to tell us about the situation, I wanted to visit him immediately, but that was just how tough the times were: you weren't even able to meet your loved ones when they probably needed you the most.

Shruti was heartbroken and felt dizzy; her mother-in-law made her lie down to calm her down. There was loss everywhere she turned—on television, social media and in every conversation—consolidating her grief. Watching the news and reading articles about deaths and people suffering invariably makes you feel bad; it hurts all the more when someone close to you goes through it all.

There were no answers as to why or how Karan got sick, and I'm sure Shruti was wondering why him, why did he have to catch this, will the treatment work, will he ever recover and come back home? I advised Shruti not to go down that unending rabbit hole of whys and wherefores, because there was no clear answer to the horrendous time she was going through. Jasmine also did her best to allay her fears. She assured Shruti that everything would be all right and that she would once again feel the joy and happiness to create wonderful memories with Karan and their child. It was only because of all the unstinting support and constant motivation from her friends and loved ones that Shruti could compose herself and feel that even this catastrophe would pass.

* * *

Karan was kept under observation in the COVID isolation ward, where the staff monitored his oxygen-saturation levels round-the-clock. His admission process had been seemingly smooth, but he was told to be prepared for up to ten days of hospitalization. Seeing the other COVID patients around him and the hospital staff in their ominous PPE kits, he wondered whether he would ever go home and see his family again. He was told that he would be tested again after a few days and until then, he would be monitored continuously. The very atmosphere of the hospital was daunting, especially because of the constant state of panic in the air.

The next day, one of the junior lady doctors visited him and he was given Remdesivir, as his condition wasn't stabilizing.

'We've given you an antiviral drug. Your condition will improve soon. I'm sure everyone here is looking after you and making sure that you recover quickly,' she said. Karan couldn't see her face as it was completely covered by the PPE kit, but the confidence with which she reassured him gave him immense relief.

'By when will I be discharged? Can't I at least talk to my family?' he asked.

'Not now . . . you need to be stable first. And don't worry, we're your family too, and will treat you as such. You can relax,' she answered with much more warmth than the aloof clinical care of a doctor. He could see her eyes through the kit, and it definitely wasn't the look that he would've expected from a doctor. Her eyes radiated an inexplicable fondness, and he couldn't stop admiring them. Karan gazed at her as she walked away from him, and when she glanced over her shoulder at him, he could sense the smile covered by the PPE kit. His mind wrestled to comprehend what had just happened as he was lost in the ecstasy of the attention her eyes had showered.

What was that? Who was she? Do I know her? The way she treated me was so different. Like we know each other. Like we had met before. Also, those eyes, that voice, everything sounded so familiar. Like I've gazed into those eyes for hours and hadn't had enough of it. It's like I've heard that voice every day and still longed for more. But why did I sense this connection so strongly? Was I hallucinating? Was my tired brain playing tricks on me or was it for real? If it had been real, who was she?

The same episode kept repeating on a loop for the next couple of days whenever they interacted, but she never revealed her identity, and Karan never asked; but every day, he waited for the moment when she would come to check on him in that affectionate manner. He even asked the nurses who she was, but they merely told him the lady doctor's designation and nothing more.

Apart from her, hardly anyone interacted with him for even a second because of the mad rush in the hospital. Every day, some nurse would administer the injections and medicines but would leave without giving him any proper instructions or updates. It was only this kind doctor who did so, and this made him very curious. That night, after her visit, Karan's condition suddenly became critical and his oxygen level, which had stabilized above 90 for the last couple of days, dropped again. He felt like he'd had a stroke and could hardly open his eyes. The nurse on duty immediately telephoned his home.

'Hello?'

Karan's mother answered the phone. It was already past 1 a.m. and she froze when she heard the phone ring. She had a sinking feeling that it was from the hospital. Ever since Karan had been admitted, the three of them hardly slept, wondering and worrying about him. They weren't even allowed to talk to him much so; they just asked the staff how he was doing once a day.

'I'm calling from KLM hospital. This is regarding your patient, Karan, who was admitted to the COVID isolation ward.'

Karan's mother trembled with dread and a chill crept into her bones as she wondered whether Karan was okay, deeply alarmed to have received a call from the hospital so late in the night. Karan's father, seated beside her, was on tenterhooks, wanting to know what the matter was.

'Yes, tell me,' his mother said, summoning up the little courage.

'We're calling to tell you that the patient's oxygen level has suddenly dropped below 90. We've increased the saturation level again. Also, his haemoglobin is low, and we need to transfuse one unit of blood, for which we need your consent.'

Karan's mother burst into tears. She did give her consent but asked, 'Is he conscious or . . .'

'He is. Don't worry. He'll be fine.'

She hung up the phone with shaking hands and narrated what the nurse had said to Karan's father.

'Have they lost their minds?' exploded Karan's father. 'If it was only about the blood transfusion, they could've called us in the morning. I got scared thinking God knows what.'

'Should we tell Shruti about this?' Karan's mother asked.

'Not now; let her sleep. She's sleeping properly today, after a long time, so don't trouble her right now,' his father responded.

Shruti was asleep and dreaming that she was standing beneath a lowering sky in pouring rain, screaming because she had lost hope, control and power. Alone and heartbroken, she was too frightened to even move her feet and felt that no one, not even she herself, could save her from this storm. With every shriek, she remembered everything she once had and everything she was about to lose, including Karan. She thought that she had lost him.

* * *

The next day, when Karan woke up, he felt much better. He had the hospital breakfast served to him and after a check-up and his daily cocktail of medicines, the nurse administered the COVID test again. He kept thinking about his family and wondered whether Shruti was taking care of herself properly.

However, his mind was still consumed by curiosity about the mysterious lady doctor, and that day, he resolved to ask the doctor whether they knew each other. His eyes were glued to the door of the intensive care ward a few minutes before her visit was scheduled. Every time the door swung open, he looked up expectantly hoping to catch a glimpse of her, but it was only the ward staff coming in or going out. He didn't know why he was so curious about her and what drew him to her or gave him such an adrenaline rush.

Eventually, the door opened, and she walked in. He noticed that the moment she stepped in, her eyes sought him out first among all the other patients in the ward. This wasn't the first time that this had happened in the last few days; but the more it occurred, the more he felt the inexplicable tug of a strong connection.

'How are you feeling today?' she asked.

'Good,' he replied, his gaze fixed on her; his curiosity growing by the second.

She looked at his reports and said, 'The nurse told me that you had some breathing problems last night. I just got your CT scan report and the patches that had formed on your lungs have reduced substantially. Now, we're just waiting for your COVID report.'

He didn't bother to ask her about his health and before he could lose his nerve, he said, 'Doctor, do we know each other? I mean, ever since the first day, I felt that I've seen those eyes before and have heard this voice. Some connection, maybe?' She raised her eyebrows and Karan felt he ought not to have asked. To cover up his faux pas, he said, 'I am sorry if I've overstepped a line. I was just curious.'

'No . . . not at all.' A smile appeared on her face, and she removed her face shield but kept her mask on. 'In fact, I'm surprised it took you so long to ask if we knew each other.'

He saw her for the first time. She had such warmth in her eyes that even an iceberg would've melted. Karan was stunned. He couldn't utter a complete sentence without stuttering and stammering. So many words jostled in his brain that he could've screamed, but he was tongue-tied. After all, she was his first love; the first romantic relationship he'd ever had.

She smiled gracefully and added, 'Of course, we had a connection. That too, a strong one. I thought you forgot. But no . . . you still remember . . . just by my voice and eyes. Impressive.'

'Navya . . . how come you're here? I can't believe my eyes,' he exclaimed.

'Why? Don't I look like a doctor to you?'

'No . . . not like that. I didn't expect you here.'

'Oh yeah, I've been a junior doctor in this hospital for the past two years. Anyway, you take care. I'll talk to you later; more often now that you've recognized me.' She winked at him and pulled on her face shield again.

When she was done with her rounds, she turned and glanced at him one last time before leaving the ward. Her eyes radiated the same inexplicable fondness that he had seen on the first day, because of which he hadn't been able to stop admiring them. They looked into each other's eyes a bit longer every day. He clung to the remnants of nostalgia—faint recollections of their first kiss, the first time they had held hands and walked in the park, their first date. The memories flooded Karan's thoughts in that moment and time lost all meaning. But the next moment he realized that a lot of water had passed under the bridge, and maybe, like him, she could be married to someone. Perhaps she was a mother. Nevertheless, a smile still lingered on his lips.

The past few years have flown by so quickly! It seems like only yesterday that we were declaring our undying love for each other. I never thought that seeing you after so many years would arouse emotions in me just as it did then. Ideally, I shouldn't feel this way now that I'm happily married, but I don't know why . . . I have no justification . . . maybe, it's rightly said, you never forget your first love, he thought.

Navya talked to him easily and comfortably, like the ghost of their past love wasn't hovering over them. Their love had been beyond any superficial infatuation, and hence, he had let her go. Had it been an egoistic obsession, she would've been in his arms. Both Navya and Karan's parents had opposed their relationship because they didn't belong to the same caste, and neither Karan nor Navya wanted to go against their families. They parted ways and moved on with their lives, only to meet again when they least expected it. Karan's test result came back negative and as soon as the formalities were done, Dr Navya came to see him, to give the instructions which he needed to follow after his discharge.

'Congratulations, your test result is negative. You've won the battle against COVID.' Although the nurse had already revealed this to him, Navya's words soothed his heart.

Karan looked at her glowing face and said, 'No. It wasn't just me; we—we won the battle. I couldn't have done it alone. It was because of your staff who took such good care of me and made sure I made it out of the woods successfully.'

'Oh . . . so, does the credit just go to the staff?' Navya pulled a mock disappointed face.

Karan rephrased his gratitude, 'And you, of course, you, who instructed them. Thank you.'

Navya grinned and told him all the necessary precautions and steps he was supposed to follow.

'Welcome to your second life,' she said.

Karan pondered over what she meant by second life; but soon after, he was discharged, and he was back in his happy place. His parents had come to pick him up and their happiness knew no bounds to see him hale and healthy again. At one point, he had thought he would never see them again. The moment he reached home, he embraced Shruti like there was no tomorrow. They melted in each other's arms; they had longed to feel each other's touch. Karan touched her stomach to feel their baby growing inside her. All these days without him, Shruti had been living for her child, so that her grief didn't affect her child's health. But after seeing Karan again in front of her, she felt alive again.

Karan's parents asked him to rest and left them alone. Shruti made him lie down. She pampered him, expressing her feelings after so long and then went into the bathroom to change into her night clothes. Karan had just closed his eyes when he received a WhatsApp message notification. It was from an unknown number.

Hi, this is Navya. Got your number from patient details. I just finished my duty and thought of messaging to ask you about your health. As I did every day. Hope you're feeling better now. There might be some residual weakness, but you'll soon feel energetic again. Take care. Goodnight.

He didn't know how to react. He gave a guilty start, thinking about Shruti. But when he saw that she was still in the bathroom, he glanced at the profile picture.

Seems to be at some conference she might have attended, he assumed.

She was still online, and seeing that, he quickly typed a message before Shruti could see him texting.

Slight weakness, but all good. Thanks for asking. Goodnight. Ttyl.

After sending her the text, he saved Navya's number under a fake name and immediately deleted the chat so that Shruti wouldn't get suspicious reading it. His mind still dwelt on her last words, 'Welcome to your second life.'

Chapter 8

Two weeks later

As per the fresh guidelines, the lockdown had eased up zone-wise; the flights had restarted and things were gradually returning to their normal routine. For those of us, like Karan and our group, who had gone through a harrowing time with illness, hospitalization and death of loved ones, COVID was brutal; but for those who merely experienced it second hand, only hearing and reading about the spread of the lethal pandemic via the media, it was a scam. Some people were still scared stiff, while others blithely made plans for their vacations after the unlock.

Unfortunately, the easing of restrictions didn't bring me any solace as bookstores were still shut in most areas, and the malls hadn't re-opened either. I had already submitted my book but there was still no clarity on when the publishers could release it. Jasmine had quit her job, and although it had been a mutually agreed decision by both of us, somewhere deep inside, the anxiety about our survival was killing me. We had broken into our nest egg of savings, which was fine, but the question remained: how long could we keep this up? I knew that in the second half of this year, there would be no royalties, as there had been no sales in the first half of the year. And when everything re-opened, would the book market still be the same?

The world was seeing a transition; people were struggling to make ends meet and didn't know when their suffering would end. In such a situation, would anybody want to relax with a book? Weird thoughts attacked my mind every day and my outlook and behaviour changed so drastically that I lacked the motivation to even do my daily chores. Jasmine began to sense that something was troubling me badly and asked me several times, but I brushed aside her questions, saying it was nothing serious. In reality, the apprehensions were crashing and thrashing their way into my mind, consuming me from the inside out.

All I needed to do was talk to those close to me, who cared for me, and tell them what I was going through; but my anxieties were in the driving seat and they trusted no one.

Neerav and Jasmine had planned to meet at Karan's home that day after dinner, and although I wasn't really keen, I decided to join them.

'We're so happy to see you smiling again. You look so much better now than you did in the initial couple of days after your discharge,' said Jasmine smiling, when we sat together in Karan's room, having our drinks.

'I think that's a fake smile because he isn't allowed to drink,' Neerav mocked them. 'See, Shruti's wearing a similar smile.'

'That's not the reason. In that hospital, I was almost sure that my time was over. So, it feels good to see you guys drinking again.'

Neerav looked meaningfully at me and commented, 'Isn't it strange that the hosts aren't drinking and the guests are already half a bottle down?'

I laughed; there was something special about these guys because they made me forget my worries whenever we were together.

Shruti got up and said, 'I'll bring some popcorn.'

'Wait, I'll join you.' Jasmine went along with her to the kitchen. Karan's parents were already asleep in their room.

'So how was your experience in the hospital? You didn't tell us,' I asked Karan, sipping my drink.

As I fixed my next peg, Karan answered, 'Don't ask. I didn't want to tell you in front of Shruti and Jasmine, but it was horrible. There was an incident on the third day, I think, one of the patients in the ward passed away. Now, obviously, we aren't used to seeing deaths every day, but the medical staff were just chit-chatting casually by my bed saying, *"panchi tha, ud gaya"* . . . like it was just a joke. A bird that just flew away. I thought, after a few days, they would be saying the exact same thing about me.'

Karan was very serious when he narrated this incident, but both Neerav and I exchanged glances and then burst out laughing. I don't know if we were already high, but we had never heard death being described like this before.

We carried on with our drinking session and after some time, when Shruti had gone to sleep, Karan received a message.

Had a long day. Just got free. What're you doing? It was from Navya.

Nothing. Just sitting around with friends at home. Was just telling them about my hospital experiences.

You mean you were telling them about our meeting? she sent a winking emoji along with the message.

Karan just sent a smiley emoji in return, to which Navya replied, *Don't drink. You're still in the recovery phase.*

I know, don't worry, Karan texted her back.

He was so engrossed in his phone that Neerav got pissed off and demanded, 'Who're you chatting with at this hour. Shruti is already sleeping. Did you meet some girl in the hospital?'

Karan immediately deleted the chat and reacted, 'What nonsense! Don't talk rubbish.'

'Don't start fighting again,' Jasmine pleaded. 'It's already too late. Let's wrap up.'

I was drinking my pegs way too fast, and she had noticed it. 'Aditya, will you please drink slowly? Or just wind up?'

'I'm in control,' I growled truculently. 'Don't tell me what to do and what not to. I'm sane enough to understand.'

The moment I uttered those words, both Neerav and Jasmine decided to pack it in and go home. I tried to convince them that all was well and that we could sit for a while longer, but they were determined to call it a day. Karan took the hint and announced that he was sleepy, and eventually, we left.

When I stood up, I realized I was actually drunk. Both Neerav and Jasmine suggested we hire a cab and not drive, but I was too far gone to listen to them.

'This is now happening regularly . . . henceforth, I will not join you guys!' declared Jasmine, infuriated by my behaviour.

I was barely able to stand but was still high on confidence. 'Don't start, please. All I'm saying is that I'm not drunk but you guys don't believe me. I'm going and if you want to come with me, let's go.'

I climbed into the car and slammed the door shut. Neerav was very worried, seeing this scene play out in front of him and said, 'Call me as soon as you reach home.'

Jasmine sat in the car in a mutinous silence, and I raced home. She gripped the dashboard in front of her with one hand and hung on for her dear life to the handle above her window. She gaped at me in terror, but I kept driving without looking at her, concentrating on the empty road ahead. She waited for a few seconds before saying something, thinking I would reduce the speed on my own, but when I didn't, she shouted, 'What kind of madness is this? You're already drunk and you're driving way too fast. Please, slow down!'

I kept quiet and gradually eased off on the accelerator. But she was too upset, and I was too drunk.

'I am telling you, Aditya, if you do such things again, I'll go back to Delhi. I will leave you.'

'If you want to leave, then go. But I won't leave you. I love you.' I tried to calm her down with my drunken logic. But it didn't go down too well, and she raised her voice further.

'Are you even serious about your life? You're in your thirties now, Aditya, and you behave like you're in fuckin' college.'

Unable to take it any more, something snapped, and I screamed back, 'What should I do to make you stop talking shit? I'm obviously serious and that's why I'm fuckin' pissed off thinking about the future—our future.'

'Is this how you think about our future? Great! Amazing!' she said sarcastically, with a slow clap, which only annoyed me even more.

'Yeah, great . . . you'll never understand what I'm going through.'

'Should it always be me who should understand? And what are you supposed to do? Nothing.'

A tense silence filled the close confines of the car for the next few minutes until we were almost home. I turned my head sideways to look at her.

Seeing her despondence, I said, 'I'm doing everything I can. I think you're just looking for an excuse—any excuse—to leave me. And if that is so, then give me my money and go and live happily.'

'Money? What money are you talking about?' she raised her eyebrows.

'Nothing.'

'No, tell me. What did you mean?' she repeated.

'I said nothing, and I don't want to talk about it now.' I myself didn't know why I had uttered those words; but I immediately sensed that I had said something terribly wrong.

As soon as we got home, Jasmine didn't walk into the bedroom. I had neither the will nor the energy to cajole her. I crashed on my bed, and she sat in the living room and wept. My actions and attitude had affected her deeply. Sitting alone, she wondered what was actually going wrong in our relationship, but she couldn't figure it out. How could she, when I had never confided in her? But it was my reticence that tore us apart and neither of us realized it.

Conflicts are undoubtedly inevitable in any relationship, but that night, her self-respect was shattered. She barely knew what to do. She was numb, sitting all alone. After crying for hours, she made her decision and texted me.

I don't know how to tell you this, but I believe it's essential that I should communicate it to you here and now otherwise we'll never move past this, and we'll just keep drifting apart ... silently

I never expected you to treat me this way. Your hurtful words keep echoing inside my head, destroying me over and over again. This is not the first time that I've told you to drink in limit, but you choose to not take it seriously. If

I forgive you again, you'll only repeat the same thing again. You made a promise. You vowed to never do it again. Why couldn't you honour your promise?

Today, my mind is clear. I had to say everything that has been weighing me down. I know things haven't been perfect lately—for both you and me. But have you really forgotten all the good times? Have you forgotten the years we spent making each other laugh, and you loving me even in the worst of times?

It's not just today's fight; it's like we've created a chasm between us but neither of us has the guts to even acknowledge the elephant in the room, let alone deal with it. That's why I've made a decision. I won't stay with you. I don't know where I will go, but I definitely cannot be with you until you realize the error of your ways. Goodbye, Aditya. Before you read this message, I'll be gone. Take care of yourself. And remember, I still love you.

Her heart had been repeatedly and relentlessly pulverized. Rather than trying to mend the fences yet again, she decided to leave. If there's anything worse than a broken heart, it is that you never saw it coming.

* * *

The next day, when I got up, I had a terrible hangover. I checked my watch and discovered that it was already past noon.

Damn, I had an important call in the morning. Why didn't Jasmine wake me up? I thought.

I got up and drank the water that was kept beside the bed. Jasmine wasn't in the room, and to check on her,

I went out into the living room. She wasn't there either. She was nowhere in the house.

I initially assumed she had gone out to buy something, but then vague memories of last night's debacle came back to me. I remembered her saying something about leaving me. Startled, I darted around like a panicking animal and fished out my mobile with its charging cord. Unfortunately, its battery had drained out completely as in my drunken stupor I had forgotten to switch on the charging button. Insecurity poured through me like scalding water, and I immediately charged the phone. All the notifications pinged open, and it was only then that I read the heartbroken message that Jasmine had sent.

I felt like screaming, I wanted to rip my heart out. I cradled my head in my hands, tears dripping through my fingers. My vision was blurred; my senses were so overwhelmed that I felt like I was suffocating; my head was pounding and intrusive thoughts echoed in my ears.

I immediately telephoned her with shaking hands, hoping against hope that she would answer the call, but her phone was not reachable. I tried again, but got the same response. Tidal waves of terrifying thoughts crashed down on me, trying to drag me under, away from my sense of self into an endless void. I called Neerav to ask if he had any idea where Jasmine was.

'I don't know. But, yesterday, before leaving, you both were arguing a lot,' he replied.

'Was I very drunk?' I asked him.

'Yes, you were. She didn't want you to drive, obviously she cares for you. But you were in a different zone altogether.'

Jasmine wasn't fighting with me; she was fighting for me, and I was a fool to not listen to her, I said in my mind.

'Fuck, man, I shouldn't have had so much.' I told Neerav all that had happened and all that I could remember. When I told him that I didn't know where she was, he revealed the truth.

'Shit, did she seriously go to Delhi?'

'Delhi?' I couldn't wrap my head around what he was saying.

'Yes. After you guys reached home and you were dead to the world, she called and told me everything you said. She was extremely upset and crying, as she hadn't expected such behaviour from you. She even said that there's something troubling you, but for some reason, you aren't telling her.'

'It's not that . . . it's just—' I began, but he stopped me.

'Don't interrupt me . . . first, listen to me. Now, I don't know what it was, but she said that if she forgives you this time, your relationship will be ruined. I tried to convince her not to go to Delhi and told her that she could go to your parents' home if she wanted; but she didn't want to involve parents in this. Obviously, you are both mature adults, so why trouble parents? But I thought I had persuaded her to not go to Delhi. She did tell me that she had booked her ticket, but after our talk, she agreed not to go. Now that you're saying she isn't here, she must've taken the early morning flight that she had booked. By now, she must have reached her home.'

I was shell-shocked to hear this. After hanging up, I texted her.

I know I've hurt you. I've said things that I'm not proud of. I am sorry. Do you think we can put this behind us? Trust me, not even a thousand apologies can express how awful I feel. It wasn't my intention to make you feel unworthy. Please, let's not forget the beautiful moments we've shared together over one bad day. I wish I could erase last evening from our memories entirely. I'll tell you what I'm going through. My insecurities. But promise me you'll always be here for me. Please come back. Please talk to me. It has only been a few hours, but it feels like eternity. I cannot live like this. I want you here beside me. You were right; I am indeed an idiot, but this idiot loves you beyond measure.

A few hours had passed, and I felt more restless with every passing minute because I was unable to reach her. I called her mother as a last resort. I casually chatted with her, but when I asked her if she could give the phone to Jasmine, Jasmine refused, saying she would talk to me later. I knew she was avoiding me on purpose, but I was helpless, thousands of kilometres away from her. I kept trying to call her every few minutes in the hope she would change her mind, but gradually, I began to lose all hope; I was losing myself. I wanted her to come back, and I was ready to do absolutely anything she asked of me.

After some time, Karan called to say that he wanted to meet me urgently as he wanted to tell me something. I assumed it was about Jasmine, but when I asked him what it was, he said that it was about the turmoil he was going through in his life. I felt he was more than serious by his tone. I instantly agreed to meet him, despite my own inner turmoil.

I picked him up from his home, and as I was driving the car, he shared his dilemma with me. When he did so, I was stunned because I knew without an iota of doubt that Shruti, and only she, was the right person for Karan.

'*Bhai*, relationships are not like sitcoms, with a different plot every week. It's the same story with the same person. Are you doubting whether you've married the right girl or not, at this juncture, now, when you're about to become a father?' I demanded, trying to read his mind. We were in the car, and while the traffic on Godbunder Road near my house was already irritating me, his revelation really got my goat. I tried to concentrate on the road, but my thoughts were focused on him. He was always texting someone on his phone and now I was sure he was chatting with the same girl he had just been talking about.

I patiently waited for his response. He eventually turned to me and scowled, 'Did I say that? I can't stop myself. I'm attracted to her. I still care for her—because I'm human, with sensitivities, empathies and weaknesses, which I wish I could overcome; because it's possible to still have feelings for someone, even if that person treated you badly in the past; because feelings don't just go away because we want them to. It wasn't intentional. It just happened after we met coincidentally.'

'I think you have lost it totally, Karan.'

I was annoyed but he pleaded, 'Please, listen to me.'

'Okay ... go on.'

He took a deep breath, 'So, we met, as I said, coincidentally, and then started talking to each other on the phone. Whenever I got a chance, I went down to call her, making excuses about going for a walk as the doctors had suggested. At other times, we interacted on messages, and I would delete the chats immediately. We never met after that. But I know she's divorced because her ex-husband never cared for her, and that she still likes me and wants to be with me, so I'm in a dilemma. Memories of her haunt my dreams. I want to meet her and at least talk to her.'

'And then what? Be in a relationship with her? And have you said anything about it to Shruti?' I asked, shifting gears as I finally saw a clear stretch of road ahead.

'Of course not. It's only you that I am sharing this with.' His face dropped, knowing he was caught in a fix.

It's said that love is like old wine. But if your old love comes back into your life, that same old wine can give you a terrible hangover that you can't get rid of for the rest of your life.

'Look, I understand, but here we are not talking about you just missing your ex or having a soft corner for her in your heart.' I was making him understand the consequences of the step he wanted to take. 'You actually want her to be in your life and that's bullshit.' My tone rose, 'Come on, Shruti loves you so much. Even you love her, we all have seen that warmth in your relationship. And now, when you are about to take a new step in life, you are making a mess of it. This is the time she needs you the most. She is pregnant. Have you thought of what would happen if she got to know all this crap?'

'That's the whole point. It's still not too late, and I don't want any regrets later,' Karan said in a perplexed voice.

He couldn't have asked for anyone better than Shruti, but here he was, sitting beside me, debating whether he should go back to a girl who never really cared for him.

Karan was wholly preoccupied as I continued driving. I could gauge his thoughts to an extent. Nevertheless, I couldn't ignore the tornado of panic swirling inside me regarding Jasmine that I hadn't shared with Karan yet, as I felt it wasn't the right time. I had actually wanted to confide in him that evening, which was why I had arranged to meet him, but considering his present state of mind, I felt it would be better to keep my problems to myself for the time being.

I touched his shoulder to snap him out of his reverie, 'You know, there'll always be a spark left in the heart. You don't need to put it out completely; nevertheless, it's always better to keep such flames under a fire blanket, otherwise they could burn down your entire house.'

'Now don't get into author mode with me. I genuinely want you to help me out in this situation.'

'What the fuck am I supposed to do? It's not a novel in which I frame the incidents according to my wish and will. You're the one who has to make the decision. And I've already told you what I think. Like you said, it's still not too late and, trust me, I too don't want you to have any regrets later.'

'Maybe,' said Karan, 'maybe I will regret it; but will it kill us to try? To put in every bit of effort? I mean, this is our life we're talking about. We don't just walk away when things get difficult, right?'

His words struck me like a bolt of lightning. In the last twenty-four hours, my life had turned upside down when Jasmine walked out—leaving our house and leaving me. It was my fault, and I was guilty. But she had just walked away without giving me a chance to explain. And here I was, giving relationship advice to my friend when my own relationship was badly fucked up. We had been married for three years and it wasn't that we hadn't had arguments before; but this was beyond serious, and all I could do was bitterly blame myself for it. Only yesterday, I had posted our picture on Instagram and everyone had told us that our relationship was like a fairy tale. But what people tend to forget is that, in real life, relationships require much more than those lovey-dovey pictures that are uploaded on Instagram. Just as every other couple did, we too had our conflicts, but we kept those to ourselves. I wished I could erase that episode and rewrite it as I do in my books—but life doesn't have a backspace button.

I picked up the phone that I had placed on the dashboard, and with one hand still on the steering wheel, I re-dialled Jasmine's number. This was the umpteenth time I was calling her in the past few hours, hoping she would talk to me at least once and give me a chance to clarify things. Her phone remained unreachable.

I opened our WhatsApp chat and my gaze switching between the road ahead and the mobile screen, I texted her, 'Why are you doing this? You know I didn't mean to hurt you. Please call me back.'

I didn't realize that I had jumped a red light at the roundabout in that moment and a car, which was hurtling towards us from the right, almost rammed into us. I yanked up the emergency brake and our car screeched to a halt. I snapped back to my senses at the close call. As I rested my head on the steering wheel, I realized that my negligence could have proved fatal for both Karan and me. Karan had braced himself against the dashboard to avoid slamming into it. His screams to me to stop at the red light had fallen on deaf ears.

'What the fuck are you doing, dude? Are you all right?' he shouted.

Everything wasn't all right. Neither with him, nor with me and neither of us knew how to untangle the chaos we were trapped in.

After spending some time together, I dropped Karan off at his colony's gate. The moment I dropped him and left, he called Navya.

'How are you, Navya?' he asked, sounding more confident about taking things forward.

'I'm fine. What's up? You sound happy today,' she guessed by his tone.

'Yes, because I have an answer to your question today,' Karan replied. His heart skipped a beat.

'Really?' said Navya, delighted to hear the optimism in his voice.

'Yes, but not now. Let's meet tomorrow. I'll make some excuse at home and come to meet you. Just you and me.'

'I'll be waiting. In fact, I've been waiting for this moment for a long time,' Navya expressed her emotions.

'See you then,' Karan hung up.

While Karan was being delusional and digging his own grave, I was trying to sort out the mess in my life. I decided to go to Delhi. To reassure myself that my decision was right, I called Neerav and told him.

'Did you try calling her parents?' he asked.

'I did. I tried every way possible, but nothing worked. She doesn't want to talk to me on the phone. I called my mother-in-law twice, but both times, Jasmine refused to talk to me and told her mom to tell me she would call me later. Now what am I supposed to do? If I call again, her mother will become suspicious.'

'That's true. And anyway, she did say she doesn't want to involve parents. If you reveal something to them, it will only lead to more complications.'

'Exactly. That's why I've decided to go to Delhi and convince her.'

'You're right. And it's better you go to her rather than just sit here, cajoling and coaxing her on the phone or texts. I'm sure she'll be more than happy to see you in Delhi.'

'I hope so too.'

Chapter 9

One of Karan's feet was on his future path, the path that led to happiness; but the other was pulling him into his past, where he had suffered heartbreak before. He was at a crossroads, with two lives before him. One pushed him into the land of prospects and the other held him back, like he had unfinished business. Memories held him back, but new ambitions drew him forward. Uncertainty had enveloped him in a swirling, distorted fog of mixed emotions, rendering him unable to gauge what was right and what wasn't. That night, he tossed and turned in bed, unable to sleep; he had promised Navya that he would meet her, and she had taken the day off especially for him. However, from one isolated corner of his heart, he could hear a plaintive voice dissuading him from treading this path. He did his utmost to hide his emotions from day one and tried to not dwell on that which he was hiding, but it kept hitting him like a dark wave. He lay on his bed, trying to find composure.

What's happening to me? Why am I drawn to her like this against my better judgement, even though there are times when I want to break away? I really don't know what the future holds for us. Although there are no issues with my married life, all of a sudden I feel a deep affection for Navya. Does one really need to have issues or complications in one's marriage to feel love for another woman? Is monogamy absolutely necessary for a happy and fulfilling relationship? Do we really need to have a hardship in marriage? And if so, why are my feelings pulling me towards her? Was I delusional in thinking that Shruti was my true love all this while? And then I met Navya again only to suddenly develop the same love-like feelings for her? Am I delusional now, thinking Navya is the one? Was I wrong all these months to think what I felt for Shruti was love and that was what I needed, or am I wrong now when I feel that wasn't the real deal? Suddenly, my brain is cranking out feelings for both of them. Even now, when I look at Shruti, a calmness surrounds me, like I am secure beside her. Nevertheless, I feel an urge to explore the sea of ecstasy and break those walls of security around me.

With these myriad bewildering thoughts, Karan didn't know when he dozed off. The next morning, when he got up, he immediately checked to see where his phone was. He had plugged it in to charge and feared Navya might have called or messaged when Shruti was around. Luckily for him, there were no notifications from her.

He freshened up and sat down for breakfast. Shruti said, 'I hope you didn't forget that today we have an appointment with the doctor.'

Karan was startled, thinking she was talking about Navya. 'Doctor? Which doctor?'

'What kind of a question is that?' she laughed. 'Obviously, our gynaecologist. Who else?'

'Oh, shit. I totally forgot to tell you that today I have to go to the hospital for a check-up. There are specific dates on which I have to go, and today is one of them. They'll check my haemoglobin, CRV value and other stuff,' Karan lied glibly, grabbing a perfect opportunity.

'Why didn't you tell me earlier? I could've postponed the appointment,' Shruti was disappointed. 'Anyway, what time will you be back?' she asked.

'I don't know. Depends on how much time it takes. Could be a few hours,' Karan lied again.

'I'll come along with you. No need to go alone,' she said decisively. Shruti was worried about his travelling alone because he was still convalescing.

However, Karan's heart was in his mouth to hear this. He wasn't good at lying, but somehow gathered the courage to speak confidently.

'No ... no ... I'll go alone. I can't risk your being in a COVID hospital. I'll go in a cab. And also, don't cancel your appointment. You can go with Aai.'

His prompt refusal to accompany her didn't go down well with Shruti. She stared at him, wondering whether something was wrong. Karan noticed it and covered up, 'Don't worry, I'll be fine and will keep you informed.' He squeezed her hand reassuringly under the table. His parents were seated in front of them. Shruti agreed, and he felt relieved.

After breakfast, he was rummaging through his wardrobe for the perfect outfit, unable to decide, when Shruti saw his perplexed look and asked, 'What's making you think so much? Wear any shirt and go so that you can come back early. You're only going to the hospital and not on a date.'

She chuckled at her own statement, but Karan looked at her, his face deadpan. He wondered how she could so easily read his mind and fervently hoped she wouldn't get to know what he was up to.

'Funny . . . should I laugh?' he faked a grin. 'We hardly ever go out these days with the lockdown and my health. So, now that I'm going out, I should wear something good so that I feel positive at least.'

Shruti, standing beside him, holding the door of the wardrobe, quipped, 'Feel whatever you want, but please . . . don't feel positive. Stay negative.'

'Idiot. I didn't mean COVID positive. Positive in general. Damn, man, the idea of staying positive has gone for a toss after COVID!' he laughed too.

Shruti peered into his wardrobe and extracted a grey shirt and gave it to Karan, whispering, 'Wear this. You look sexy in this. Every time you wear it, I feel like kissing you right away. It just suits you so well.' She kissed his cheeks and tried turning his face towards her with her hand to kiss his lips, but Karan resisted. He felt awkward as he visualized Navya feeling the same and kissing him.

'What?' Shruti asked, surprised.

'Nothing. I was thinking of something else. Sorry,' he said and drew her close. 'Come here . . .'

Shruti pushed him away this time and said, 'Now leave . . . and come home soon.'

Karan smiled. He changed quickly. He called Navya the moment he left the house and asked her to pick him up from a junction that was some distance away from his home. He had told Navya that he wouldn't be able to bring his car, so she was already on her way.

Karan was nervous, his heart beating faster. All the while, as he stood there waiting for her, he kept scanning the area to ensure there was no one known around. He had stopped differentiating between right and wrong and just went with the flow. When Navya drew up, she leaned over and opened the door for him, and Karan quickly got inside. As soon as he was in, neither of them quite knew what to say. The blush on Navya's face made Karan realize she was just as nervous as he was and that, strangely enough, put him at ease. He gave her a sidelong glance. This was the first time in years he was seeing her in an informal attire. She looked as gorgeous as ever, natural and elegant. Her make-up wasn't overdone. Her skin still had the same glow, apart from the shadow of dark circles beneath her eyes. Navya carefully took out a small tiffin-box from her bag and gave it to him. She had made gulab jamun for him, knowing that he loved them.

'I hope they are still your favourite,' Navya said as she drove on the empty roads.

'Very much so.' Karan beaned. He was touched that she had taken out time to make it for him, especially considering how busy doctors were because of the pandemic. He felt like kissing her all over. Navya could feel his eyes on her, and she would have paid good money to hear the thoughts going through his head right then.

'You said yesterday you have the answer to my question. I'm still waiting,' she said after parking the car on the side of the road.

'You still look beautiful in these casual tops and shorts.'

She had worn it on purpose, knowing Karan loved her in such attires.

'And you still admire me the same way you used to.' Her cheeks turned red. She looked up and said, 'This shirt looks good on you. And by the way, this three-day-beard look that you are sporting these days makes you look manly. I love it.'

'Oh, thanks. Shruti loves it and so I keep it that way,' he replied instantly without thinking it through. Navya didn't react, so he added, 'I am sorry. I didn't mean to hurt your feelings.'

'No . . . not at all. Why should I feel bad?' Navya moved to face him, leaning back against the car door. 'She's your wife, after all. I could've been in her place, but it's my fault that I'm not. So, there's nothing for you to feel bad about.'

Karan gave her a reluctant smile. After a moment's silence, Navya repeated her question again, 'You said you had an answer. What is it?'

Karan had deliberately changed the topic, not knowing where to start and how. He took a deep breath and looked straight into those eyes that still held affection for him. 'Look, I've always loved you. You preferred to walk away because of your parents, and I didn't force you to stay. What could I have done when you didn't want to be with me? I'll not ask why you got divorced or what happened between you two. I understand that sometimes, some decisions in life go wrong. But before I say anything else, I want to tell you that it's not that I don't love my wife. I really do. In fact, we're expecting a baby, as I've already told you. And we're happy together. There's nothing wrong between us; it's not like she doesn't care for me and I'm trying to find solace in another woman's arms.'

Navya couldn't bear to hear any more and stopped him. 'So, do you mean to say there's nothing left between us, and you no longer have any feelings for me?'

'When did I say that? Please let me finish, before you start jumping to conclusions.' Karan closed his eyes for a moment and then, summoning up all the courage he had, he revealed his feelings, 'Despite all that I've said, I still have strong feelings for you. Now, I don't want you to ask me how I can possibly love two women simultaneously because I'm also trying to figure this out. I just know that I feel really good talking to you, almost as if you're the one I've always wanted to be with; I don't know if it's because we had a fairly strong relationship once. Whatever it is, if today I still crave to meet and be with you, hold your hand, hug you and feel your warmth . . . what does that mean? It isn't clear.'

Navya heard him out and when he was done, she said, 'Karan, why are you stressing so much? Am I telling you to be in a relationship with me or to marry me? No . . . I very well understand your position and I know how much it hurts when you put an end to your married life. I never got the love I deserved. I always kept thinking how my life would have been if I would have stood strong and married you.'

Karan interrupted her, 'But there's no point in thinking about that now.'

Navya nodded in agreement. 'I know, but I'm not saying that we should start canoodling in parks like teenagers.'

Karan didn't know how to react. Navya drew close and held his hand. She could feel his palm sweating in nervousness and she smiled. Her smile still held the same disruptive energy that could stir up storms in a serene place.

She entwined her fingers with his and said, 'I just want to be with you; spend time with you and share my things with you as a companion . . . I don't need commitments. And don't get me wrong. I don't mean I crave intimacy. I just crave emotions that have dried completely in my life. Like a machine, I start working when the sun rises and switch off when the night arrives. Will you be with me as my emotional shield? I love you, Karan.'

The distance between them had decreased further as she moved closer to him. Her every word was a husky whisper now. She had missed him so much all these years. Before Karan could respond, there was a sharp rap on the window. Navya straightened up immediately.

Two police officers on their squad motorbike gestured to her to roll down the window. Karan had been so lost in her mesmerizing eyes and voice that he hadn't even noticed them standing there.

She rolled down the window and asked them if there was something wrong. Karan was horrified for a second, pierced by the sharp sword of reality. He immediately got out of the car to speak to the policemen.

What's happening here?' the policeman demanded.

'Nothing, sir. We were just talking,' Karan replied, knowing full well that the policemen didn't buy this.

'Don't you understand the prevalent situation?' the policeman demanded in a raised voice. 'Unless absolutely necessary, you're not allowed to come out. Just because the unlock phase has started, it doesn't mean you guys start necking in public places.'

Navya quietly stepped out of the car and stood beside Karan, listening to the lawman's harangue.

'Sir, you're getting it wrong. We weren't doing anything. Trust me.'

'Who's she? Your girlfriend?' the policeman asked, jerking his head at Navya.

Karan and Navya exchanged nervous glances. Karan knew that the longer he hesitated, the more suspicious the policemen would become, so he just said what popped into his mind, 'No ... she's my wife. We just came out for a breath of fresh air ... we're going home now.'

Navya looked askance at Karan. She hadn't expected him to say that. Although it wasn't true, she loved the way he had stood by her. But the sceptical policeman asked for their identity cards. Karan realized they were on the verge of getting screwed.

On seeing their identity cards, the policeman shouted, 'You think we are fools? She is Navya Mehta. And you are Karan Sawant. Both your addresses are different. How come you are husband and wife?'

Karan was prepared for this question and answered pat, 'Sir, we haven't changed her name and addresses on the IDs. Is there a rule that we should always carry our marriage certificate with us?' Karan pretended to be cool and grinned, 'Think about it—in the middle of all this, will she travel to Thane all the way from Vashi?'

Eventually, Navya showed them her medical ID and said, 'Look, I'm a doctor. If you think we were just being a public nuisance, then you're wrong. I was really tired of all the chaos at the hospital that you very well know of and took the day off. So, I came along with my husband for a ride. Please, let us go. We'll go home. Being a doctor, I do understand the situation perfectly well. I hope you understand us too.'

After some pleading and even some bribing, they finally left. Karan and Shruti got back into the car, still not completely over the shock and wondering what would've happened if they had called someone for proof. A brief silence followed as they exchanged glances, trying to gauge what the other was thinking.

Eventually, Navya said with a laugh, 'How did you get the bright idea of pretending we were married?'

Karan was still in a state of shock, 'What the fuck was the alternative? If I had said that we were just friends, they would've screwed us over.'

Navya appreciated his presence of mind and added, 'But, are we just friends or something more?'

'Navya, can we go home now? I'm sorry, but I don't feel too good.'

Navya chuckled, looking at his ashen face, 'Look at you. You look like you've just watched a horror movie.' Karan checked his face in the rear-view mirror. He did look petrified. After a few minutes, he too had a laugh.

'You haven't changed a bit,' she shook her head. 'You get scared so easily. And even when it's done, it keeps bothering you.'

'You know what…I really love the way you remember every little thing about me. Makes me think how good we were together.' Karan could actually visualize their good times together.

After they had spent some time together, Navya dropped off Karan at the same place from where she had picked him up. On the way back home, Karan reminisced about all the times they had spent together in the past. Today, after meeting Navya after so long, he hadn't been comfortable sharing the small space within the confines of the car, with only a few inches between them. He couldn't decide whether it was because he loved Shruti or because he no longer had the same feelings for Navya, because the moment she left, he longed to spend some more time with her. But it was he who had asked to leave, and now he looked back and thought of all the things he could have done differently. He could've held her hand the way she had held his; he could've moved an inch closer to her when she leaned towards him; he could've felt her touch that once meant the world to him. He called me as he walked towards his colony.

'Where are you?' he asked.

'In Delhi. All good?' I asked. I hadn't told him I was travelling to Delhi as everything had happened so quickly.

'Delhi? Why? Are Jasmine's mom and dad all right?'

'Yeah, no worries. It's a long story; I'll tell you later. I actually wanted to tell you that day, but you bombed me with your stupidity, so I didn't want to trouble you more.'

He immediately revealed, 'I met her today.'

'You can't be serious.' There was no response from his end and that's when I sensed he was. And that stunned me, 'What the fuck. You really met her? What did you tell Shruti?

He narrated the entire episode, and I couldn't help laughing at the bit where they narrowly missed getting screwed by the long arm of the law. 'Look, even destiny doesn't want you guys to be together. The universe is sending you signals, bro. Heed them and please end this madness before it's too late—I'm telling you this repeatedly.'

Karan disconnected the call.

He wondered whether it was really destiny playing a game with him.

If it was destiny that didn't want us to be together, then why, in the first place, did we cross paths again in this life?

He was still thinking about whether they were really meant to be or not. What if destiny was playing a cruel joke on them and had set them on this headlong collision course just to leave them shattered?

Chapter 10

Sometimes, something said isn't necessarily something felt. Jasmine had been telling me for some time about the way I was letting her down, but I only fully comprehended what she meant when she actually walked away. I yearned to never be apart from her, but it was my first day without her. Like really without her. And I had no idea whether things would ever be okay or sort themselves out. I didn't merely love her for who she was, I loved her for who I was when I was with her; I loved the vision of my life with her. I loved how happy I was when she was by my side, and she had never faltered or left my side ever. She was the backbone of my existence. But for the last few hours, I felt a pain that made my heart ache, a gnawing sensation that I wasn't able to handle, and it was all the more acute because of her silence.

Ever since I landed in Delhi a few hours ago, I had telephoned Jasmine repeatedly, but there had been no response. She had never been this upset before, and

I had no clue if she was just punishing me to make me realize my mistake or truly didn't want to have anything more to do with me . . . ever. If it was the latter, my entire life would collapse, and no one knew this better than me. It felt twice as bad because I incessantly preached, talked and wrote about not taking love and relationships for granted, and here I was, in the same boat as those who had taken a loved one for granted and had suffered. It felt like the world was ending and the earth was splitting into two, just as my heart did. I eventually told Neerav to call Jasmine and tell her I was in Delhi.

'Jasmine, are you at home?' Neerav asked as soon as Jasmine answered the call.

'Yes, why, what's up?' Jasmine was with her parents.

'Listen to me, and don't react in front of your parents. Aditya has come to Delhi to meet you. He landed this morning and has been trying to reach you since then. Unblock him, please, and at least have a word with him,' Neerav requested her.

'What? Where in Delhi is he right now?' Jasmine was surprised to hear that I had travelled all the way to Delhi.

'I don't know exactly, but he said he's near your house somewhere. Do have a word with him.'

Jasmine hung up and immediately unblocked me. I was continuously calling her and the moment she unblocked me, my call connected. She went into her bedroom and answered my call.

'Thank God you finally answered my call, Jasmine . . . please . . . please talk to me . . . I thought

I had lost you forever . . . but, no . . . I love you, Jasmine. Please say something . . .'

She didn't say anything and in that silence, I could hear her muffled sobs. She said, 'I unblocked you because you're in Delhi. Not because my anger has melted away. Where are you?'

Those words gave me comfort. I was determined to make her return to me. The cords of our love weren't weak enough to break so easily. Nothing in the world was more precious than her voice.

I wiped my tears and said, 'I'm outside, sitting in the park near your house. I didn't come in directly as I didn't want to involve our parents in our problems. Please come out, I want to see you . . . I want to talk to you.'

Jasmine hung up. In a few minutes, she came to the park, which was a few metres away from her parents' house. My heart skipped a beat to see her, almost as if we were meeting after many years. Her silence was roaring inside me, and although it hadn't been much more than a day, I had a sinking feeling that our long conversations, emotions and life were fading into oblivion. But it was me who had wronged her and had hurt her so deeply. I felt profoundly guilty to think of the peace of mind I had taken from her and the smile from her face. I had never waited passively for the fight to end or for her to initiate the conversation whenever we had an argument. I hated it. It made me feel uneasy. Jasmine, on the other hand, always believed in taking time to think and re-evaluate what we had said and how we had behaved and let time do its thing.

So, when she approached me, I took a step forward to hug her, but she sidestepped me and demanded, 'Why are you here? Didn't I tell you to give me space? I don't want to talk to you.'

However, her expression betrayed her desire to feel the warmth of my arms around her. Her eyes spoke volumes, telling me that she missed me as much as I missed her.

I admitted, 'I've realized my mistake. I know I've learnt my lesson the hard way; please don't make it harder for me.'

'I'm glad that you've at least realized it, but the problem is you repeat it over and over again, and I'm fed up.'

I knew, somewhere, that my apology meant nothing. But I still expressed my love for her. 'I know that, in the past, I have repeated it. I am really sorry; I know you hate the word sorry but what should I do? Unless you give me a chance to prove myself, that's all I can do. Believe me . . . My existence would cease if you weren't around. Not even for a day could I stay at that house, thinking you won't be coming back. I promise I'll tell you whatever I am going through. It's not your fault, it's mine. I should have told you way before, but I just didn't want you to go through the same. If that insecurity was destroying my inner self, how could I share that with you, only to pull you in it along with me? Because, to be honest, there wasn't, and isn't, a solution to it even now. But trust me . . . I'll not do it again.'

'Tell me, now, what is it that's troubling you? I've asked you so many times, but you just ignore me. You call me your best friend and you don't share your agony with me? What's the use, then? Tell me now, I'm all ears.' She folded her arms and looked straight into my eyes. I could see that her eyes were swollen with all the weeping and that made me feel awful. I wanted to make her smile.

So, I told her, 'Let's go home first. Are we going to sit here all day?'

She did her best to hide her smile behind pretend seriousness. My sudden visit was a surprise to her parents, but we told them that it had been a long time since I had seen them and had planned to come along with Jasmine, but had some work, so had to come a day later. They were extremely happy to see Jasmine and me together after a year. When I saw the joy in their eyes, I understood that Jasmine had been right about not involving parents. The whole day, I made attempts to win her heart, to no avail. The next day too, nothing changed and although we were under the same roof, pretending to be happy in front of her parents, we were completely broken on the inside. I didn't know if it was the lull before the storm, like a sandcastle with the tide drawing ever closer, threatening to collapse it.

* * *

After a couple of days, Karan called to tell me that he had planned to meet Navya again and clear the air between them. He wasn't able to handle living a dual life any more, hiding things from Shruti. However, he didn't want to make a clean breast of it with Shruti, for obvious reasons. He loved her and wanted to be with her for life; but at the same time, didn't want Navya to go away either.

'Bhai, you were right. I am totally fucked. Every time I get Navya's call, I move out or go into the bathroom but I'm in constant fear. I want to meet Navya and talk about all these things,' he said.

'At the risk of repeating myself, I'll say this again, Karan: you've just met once. It has hardly been a few days and you're already in this state. It's better to come clean to Shruti rather than living a lie and letting that lie get exposed later. I don't know how she'll react. But I know what it feels like when you don't live up to your partner's expectation—it's just too horrible.'

Neerav had already told him what had happened between Jasmine and me. 'I know what you're talking about, but my situation is different.'

'Whatever the situation may be, honesty is always one of the main factors in any relationship, and I don't need to tell you that. It's much better than lying to the person you love. No matter how big or small the lie is, it's still a lie and you're still keeping it from her. Put a full stop to all this.'

'I'll meet Navya and ask her clearly what she wants.'

'Why the fuck do you call me when you've already decided to go ahead with your lunacy? You did the same thing the last time as well. Even now, when I'm advising you to put a stop to this rubbish, you're talking shit. It's not about what she, Navya, wants; it's about what you want and what you already have. A happy married life. She doesn't have that and it's not going to affect her in the least, but your whole life will be a trainwreck. Why don't you understand this simple thing?'

'I do. And that's why I need to talk to her, as it's affecting me and not her. Anyway, Shruti doesn't know you're in Delhi and I'm going to tell her that I'm going to meet you. So, manage it if she calls, although I'm fairly sure she won't.'

'*Chutiya*, you'll get screwed, and you'll screw me too one day!'

Karan hung up. He had only called to notify me that I was the smokescreen for his tryst with Navya. Later, when he was getting ready, Shruti eyed him curiously as he never usually spent so much time grooming himself to met his friends. Shruti shrugged it off and walked to his side of the bed, where he had plugged in his phone to charge.

'Karan, I'm sending some pictures to your phone and resending them to me from yours. I'm unable to scroll that far down on Instagram to upload stories,' she said, reaching for the charging chord.

Karan, who had been trimming his beard in front of the bathroom mirror, rushed out in a panic. Although he had deleted all the chats from Navya, he was afraid that Navya would call as soon as she set off from her place.

'Wait . . . wait . . . I'll send it to you.' He hastily grabbed the phone before she could touch it.

'What was that? I could've done it easily.' She was surprised by his strange behaviour.

Karan always kept his phone by his side, but that day, he had forgotten to charge it and had plugged on the charger assuming that Shruti wouldn't emerge from the kitchen any time soon.

'I'll do it. Chill.' He ignored her words.

Eventually, he sent those pictures, and then hurried out of the house but not before raising a million doubts in Shruti's mind. Shruti sat alone in the bedroom, plagued by the weird thoughts triggered by Karan's oddness.

Why did he panic so much when I looked at his phone? What could it be? I've often told him to wear shoes and smart shirts when we go out with friends, but he has always brushed it aside, saying he wasn't going on a date. But now, he is dressed to kill; and even for something as mundane as a hospital appointment that day. He's so defensive these days even when I ask him something innocuous and always looks so lost when at home. Is he lying to me or hiding something from me?

According to the old adage, love and doubt can never co-exist; but what if the loved one sows these seeds of doubt? It doesn't mean that you no longer love the person; you still do and that's exactly why you're afraid of losing him. Shruti carried on with her routines, but her mind had already set out on the path of suspicion and endless conjecture.

* * *

The first showers at the end of the summer made the weather pleasant. To avoid getting drenched, they stood by the lake, huddled together beneath the small umbrella that Navya had brought along.

'I really missed you for these past couple of days. I badly wanted to message you or call you, but was afraid to do so because I thought your wife might see my texts or answer your phone. And the wait for your call made me really desperate to talk to you,' said Navya.

'Navya . . . I still don't get it. Where're we headed? What's our future? And what exactly do we want from each other? I'm not holding you responsible for our increased closeness in the past few days, because I have the same urge as you; but I really don't know what we're doing here.' Karan gazed into her eyes. The droplets of water on her skin enthralled him. The interplay of the heat and the rain had made the moment extra special.

'Sssh . . . let time decide.' She placed a slender finger on his lips. Karan felt a jolt shoot through his body. It had been years since he had felt her sensual touch; the touch which had always transported him to another world. 'Let's not bring morality in between us. As I said before, I know you're married, and you have a life. I don't want to ruin that. I told you, I just want someone with whom I can be me—and who better than you, who knows me inside out, who loved me like crazy once, who craved me like I was his only goal in life? Let things be.'

Karan was awestruck by her husky voice. The way she expressed herself blew him away. Gradually, he felt the strings of his heart loosen and give in to his temptations. Whatever came over them at that point could only be blamed on the blissful weather. She moved her fingers away from his mouth and brought her face closer to his. A chill ran down his spine as he felt her breath tease his nose. Just as she was about to press her lips against his, reality and his conscience joined forces to strike him hard and Karan pushed himself away.

'No . . . this is wrong. I can't let my emotions control me. Let's just talk.'

Navya saw the hesitation in his eyes, 'I'm sorry, I thought we just had a moment.'

'No . . . it's okay . . . it's just that . . . I really don't think this is right. I don't know . . . I feel like I shouldn't betray the girl who loves me with the girl who left me because she couldn't trust the strength of her love.'

'Don't say anything more. I don't want to force myself on you. Take your time. I seemed to have travelled back in time to those days when there was no wall between our desires and passion; the way you loved me then with no boundaries, totally forgot everything else.' Navya apologized to him once again. They spent some time together and Karan asked her to drop him home. When he reached his apartment complex's gate, he sat down on the bench at the bottom of the stairs, mulling over what he had been going through in the past few days. A fierce battle raged between his heart and mind. His mind wanted to take back control, although his heart didn't want to relinquish the reins, making it impossible for them to function harmoniously.

His mind said, 'What about "our relationship has no future" as she had once said when her parents told her not to be with you? What about all those times she told you to go away and didn't give a shit about your emotions? Why are you giving her a chance to destroy you again?'

His heart argued, 'There's much more to our connection than all this. I've nurtured our affinity for years. Such a rapport never really goes away, even if the links are broken.'

Nevertheless, his mind maintained, 'Now that you've established a rapport with Shruti, you love her wholeheartedly. You're merely nostalgic about Navya because a part of you wants to retrieve lost ground. That is unhealthy. You know it is. I could shut you down.'

His heart was truculent, 'Oh yeah? Just try shutting me down if you dare.'

His mind said, 'You know I won't. You're the driving force. But if you stop moving in that direction, if you can just stop fucking caring so much, I'll handle you. You've already moved on, but you just don't want to accept it? You do realize that you are damaging me with your constant paranoia.'

His heart started beating wildly and said, 'Do you think it's in my control? That I'm doing it on purpose? I too know that I love Shruti . . . and no one else. It's your job to not bother responding when Navya messages.'

The brain retorted, 'Don't blame me. I read the message and directed you to delete or block and end it right away. It's not me sending replies every fuckin' time. And it's pathetic! Fuck it, heart, she never wanted you and is now using you as a sop for her loneliness again.'

'There's no proof of that.'

'When did you start caring about proof and logic, my friend? That's not you and you know it.'

His heart shrank. 'I don't know it.'

'Of course, you know it. She never cared about you. And Shruti . . . she has always cared about you. She's the one who supports you. She's the one who understands you, better than you yourself and never ever questions your decisions. She has not merely accepted your family, she loves them dearly. And now, she's carrying your baby. What more proof do you need to prove that this is what you've always wanted in your life?' demanded his mind.

'Yes . . .'

'There you go. Now, shut the fuck up and go home. And never look back again.'

Karan felt relieved; he had a smile on his face. His inner voice had now made his course of action abundantly clear and with no hesitation, he replied to Navya that that was it. They would never contact or meet each other again. He was more than relieved because, before things had spiralled out of control, he had managed to overcome temptation. Shruti was reading a book in the bedroom when he walked in. He gently drew the book from her hands and set it aside before raising her to stand before him. He looked deeply into her eyes and kissed her passionately.

'I love you. I'll always be with you,' he declared.

Shruti was surprised, and although she had enjoyed the passion of his kiss, she asked, 'Why? What has happened to you all of a sudden? You look happy, for some reason.'

'Do I need a reason to express my love to my wife?' Karan pinched her cheek.

Afterwards, they sat together for a long time, giggling over little things and they talked about their baby. Karan felt like he had redeemed himself, like he had managed to push away the heavy brick that had been lodged in his chest for quite some time now. He slept soundly for the first time after so many restless nights. Shruti, however, still brooded over the morning incident, wondering whether her misgivings held a kernel of truth. Although deep within her, she was convinced that Karan would never break her trust and that she loved him unconditionally, she wanted to check his phone to make sure there were no skeletons in Karan's closet.

When Karan was fast asleep, she quietly took his mobile. Karan didn't have a passcode because he hadn't needed one prior to meeting Navya; if he suddenly decided to lock his phone, it would undoubtedly set off Shruti's alarm bells. She swiped away a few notifications and then she saw a message on his WhatsApp. It was from Navya. Karan had saved her number as 'Doctor'.

She read the text, *I'm sorry, Karan, for coming into your life again. If I hadn't met you in the hospital, my feelings for you wouldn't have resurfaced. I won't force you to be with me and I'll stand by my word. But always remember, there's one person who still loves you. I'll always cherish the moments we spent together in the past few days. Sorry to message you first. I couldn't stop myself from telling you this after reading your message. Please delete it as soon as you read it.*

Shruti felt like a knife had been inserted between her shoulder blades. The sudden jolt of pain caused tears to sting her eyes. She hoped it was just a nightmare, and that someone would wake her up and tell her that everything was okay. It was like she had been pushed into the deepest pit of hell, with no way to climb out. She sat shell-shocked, bereft and numb, surrounded by the debris of his broken promises, her love, her dignity, her trust . . . everything.

She noted the number and looked it up on Truecaller. It showed the name, 'Navya Mehta'. Her heart couldn't decide whether she should be furious because Karan had betrayed her or mourn the death of her blind trust.

Shruti couldn't sleep all night, her pillow was soaked with her silent tears.

I had a gut feeling that something wasn't right ever since this morning, but I had fervently hoped that you would prove me wrong. I had always assumed that you would never betray me because you always reassured me that you loved me. Now I'm beginning to question my own sanity. My world has imploded and I'm utterly distraught. You were my world, my husband, the father of my unborn child and you chose to betray and hurt me to a degree beyond belief. It pierces my heart to find that you've found warmth elsewhere. Wasn't my love enough for you? You lied, you cheated, you manipulated me and faked your love. I don't even know how long you have been cheating on me. I don't know why you chose to do what you have done, but it has now destroyed me completely. Do you know what it's like to feel the pain of betrayal? Yes, you do. You know this feeling well because once upon a time it happened to you. You had told me to keep things transparent between us. What happened to that transparency now? If you knew the feeling, why would you want to inflict it on me?

The next morning, when Karan woke up, he saw that Shruti was still asleep. She had dozed off fitfully only in the early hours of the morning. He checked his phone and saw that Navya's message had already been read. His heart slammed into the back of his teeth as he realized the game was up. He didn't know how Shruti would react and quaked in fear at the impending shitstorm. He didn't delete the message, knowing that that would only make matters worse. He had just got over Navya yesterday and had assumed that there would be no more complications in his life, only to wake up to the biggest shockwave of his life.

When Shruti got up, he initiated the conversation himself, rather than hiding it any more or running away from the situation.

'You read the message yesterday?' Karan asked Shruti as she walked away without uttering a word or even looking at him.

'Yes, and I'm glad I did. At least I came to know the truth.' She slammed the bathroom door on his face.

'We need to talk,' Karan called from outside.

'Is there anything left to talk about? Your actions have spoken a thousand words and have been more than enough to reveal your true colours.' She was heartbroken and it reflected in her voice.

Karan waited for her to come out, and the moment she opened the door, he grabbed her hand to stop her from walking away again.

But Shruti freed herself from his grip and pushed him away.

'Shruti, at least listen to me. I know I should've told you right in the beginning itself, but—'

'You're a liar. You lied every morning when you woke up. Every single morning. You've been meeting her on the sly and I'm sure you've been fucking around with that girl God alone knows since when. I wonder whether you actually went to office before the lockdown, or to some sleazy hotel room, or her home.'

'No . . . I didn't. I swear I didn't touch her. And before COVID, we never met. I saw her in the hospital and have only met her twice. She is the same girl I mentioned to you, my ex-girlfriend. Trust me, please,' Karan said in a pleading voice.

'Look who's talking about trust,' Shruti's voice dripped sarcasm. Now that Karan had revealed that Navya had been his girlfriend, she wanted some more information, 'Okay, I accept that she was your ex-girlfriend, but does that justify what you've done? Did it give you the licence to betray me . . . and "cherish the moments you spent together in the last few days" as she so eloquently puts it?' Shruti sat on the bed, waiting to hear from him.

'Of course not. I'm not justifying what I did. I agree I was wrong, and I shouldn't have met her in the first place. You did read the message, right? You saw the line about her "cherishing the moments", but she also mentions that we met in the hospital, right? I'm not lying. We weren't even in touch with each other prior to that. I am just requesting you to please sit and hear me out patiently.'

Karan narrated every detail to her from the day they had met until yesterday evening and added, 'I love you and would never want to jeopardize anything we have. I've always seen a future with you and want to give my child all the happiness in the world. I told her the same thing. I know that I broke your trust, but I also want to make everything like it was before. Please, give me a chance. After I told her yesterday that we would never contact each other, I wanted to come clean with you so that you don't hear it from anyone else. My heart bleeds because you found out about my foolishness in a way that you shouldn't have.'

'You stab me in the back and now you pretend that it is you who's bleeding? How ironic is that? Here we were, weeping and praying for your health, while you were honeymooning on cloud nine with your ex-girlfriend. Did you even think about what we were going through each and every minute of those days?' Navya's message kept swirling around in her mind.

Later, Neerav called to have a word with her and explained to her that, although Karan had been at fault, he was still untainted and loved her deeply. However, Shruti would not be pacified.

Chapter 11

No relationship is perfect; not even mine. The problem wasn't that we had countless fights. There would be a problem if we didn't argue, because you only fall out with the people you care about. And in those battles, we found reasons to love each other all the more. I still remember how excited Jasmine was to marry me. She hadn't felt even an ounce of regret, although she wept with emotion as she walked along with me, leaving her parents behind; she knew her life was going to change and was ready to make that change with me. Seeing her cry, I wasn't able to control my own tears and my friends still mock me for crying during '*vidhaai*', and I still get embarrassed. Our honeymoon was filled with fun and precious memories of us chilling around Sri Lanka together. Everything was more fun because she was with me and 'goodnight' no longer meant 'goodbye'. Walking on the beach of Bentota and eating seafood remains one of our favourite memories. Since then, we have learnt a lot about loving and accepting each other. Life is a lot more complicated now. We have parents, sisters, brothers, relatives, neighbours; but when we strip away all of the extra, it is still only Jasmine and me, together. I love that we still laugh at each other's cheesy jokes, watch crazy, mind-bending shows together, and enjoy trying new things and exploring our world together. I loved our days of being newlyweds, but I think I like our current life together better. I like us. After three years, we know each other so much better and that's why I only needed time to speak with her and make her understand. Initially, for the first couple of days, I struggled to convince her casually, but somewhere in the back of my mind, I knew that wouldn't work this time. And then an idea struck me.

I was with my mother-in-law early that morning; Jasmine was still sleeping. I thought this was the best opportunity and I told her, 'Mummy, I want to make momos today. I mean, I want to try it if you can help . . . for Jasmine, as she loves it.'

My mother-in-law was surprised and looked at me in something akin to alarm, almost as if I had proposed a plan to kidnap her daughter. After staring at me for quite a few seconds, she asked, 'What's so special about today that you're entering the kitchen?'

I was sure that Jasmine had told her that I was a dead loss when it came to cooking. I would turn the kitchen upside down looking for the gas-lighter, when it was hung on a hook right in front of me; or as soon as the water boiled, I would proudly look at her as if I had generated the heat to boil it. Apart from my expertise in cooking Maggi, all I could do expertly was cook up stories.

Now what should I tell her—that I fought with her daughter and am doing all this to bring a smile to her face? She would ignore the second half and focus on the first . . . after all, she's a mother!

'Actually . . . before marriage, when we were dating, today was the day when we met for the first time in person. And I don't know if she remembers it, but I do, and I want to make it special for her. Now, as restaurants are still closed and we can't go out anywhere, I thought this could be the best gift. Because she loves momos.'

'We can order it in if you want; home deliveries have started in Delhi.'

'No . . . she'll not allow that in the first place, and even if she does, I'll have to eat it with sanitizer chutney.'

Her mother beamed, knowing her daughter well. 'Okay, I'll chop the vegetables and get all the rest of the ingredients for the stuffing and the dough ready, and you do the rest,' she patted my back. Her expression encouraged me to accept the challenge.

I'll do the rest? I'll rest in peace. I don't have a clue about what to do with all the ingredients, I replied to her in my mind.

However, now I had no option but to sink or swim, so I watched a few YouTube videos and faithfully followed the steps demonstrated. After an hour or so, my special dish was ready, although the momos looked more like ladoos.

Wow, Aditya . . . well done. I'm sure seeing these out-of-the-world momos, she'll book me a one-way ticket to Mumbai.

I tasted one and it seemed halfway decent. That restored at least some of my confidence. When Jasmine woke up, I walked over to her and said, 'Today, I have something special for you. So special that you're going to love it.'

With time, Jasmine's anger had mollified to an extent, which I could sense, but she still didn't talk to me as fondly as she used to. Nevertheless, when she heard about the surprise, her eyes couldn't hide her eagerness, even though she gave a bland reply, 'What is it now? That too so early in the morning. I don't want your bouquets and gifts.'

I didn't say anything. I knew whenever she was more upset than usual, she deprecated my floral apologies and tributes. However, my cooking was something she wouldn't have foreseen even in her wildest dreams as I had never attempted anything like this before. My air of mystery only made her curious, and after freshening up, when she ventured into the living room, she saw momos in a tray on the dining table, with candles around it. Jasmine was pleasantly surprised to see her favourite dish but had no idea what was going on.

She looked at me and my smiling face and then turned her puzzled gaze to her mother and asked, 'What's all this, and why?'

Her mother smiled and said, 'Taste it. Aditya woke up early this morning to make it especially for you. He'll tell you why.'

She was startled to hear that and said in an overwhelmed voice, 'You made it? For me?'

'I tried to. I don't know whether you'll like it or not.'

I picked one up in my hand and brought it close to her mouth. She was still looking at me without blinking. Her moist eyes spoke volumes, a mighty happiness reflecting in them, and her anger rolled away down her cheeks as tears. My world looked colourful again. She was my comfort, but she sometimes pushed me out of the nest, out of my comfort zone, to do things I didn't know I could do. She was the spark in my life.

When she tasted it, she valiantly tried to not look disgusted.

'How is it?' I hoped she had liked it, although, going by her expression, I was being a tad optimistic.

'Do you really want an honest review?' she asked.

I nodded. My in-laws were waiting with bated breath for her reaction. She took another bite to recheck if her first evaluation was right. After gulping it down, she said, 'It's good that you don't cook food. Better you stick to cooking stories. That's your forte.'

We all looked at each other and then burst out laughing. But Jasmine appreciated me saying, 'However, I loved that you put in the effort.'

'Beta, at least remind her of the reason for your making it,' my mother-in-law prompted me, and I remembered the story I had fabricated this morning.

Jasmine was baffled. I looked sheepish, 'I told her why today was special. We had met for the first time today. So, I tried to make it special.'

Jasmine knew that was a white lie, but she didn't expose my duplicity. I didn't care whether she liked my cooking or not, what mattered was she understood my rationale.

Later that evening, when her parents had gone out for a stroll, I went into the bedroom and took out the gift I had hidden in my bag. She was in the living room, watching a web series. I asked her to close her eyes.

'This is something which is very close to your heart and an apology to you for whatever happened. I promise I won't ever do that again. This will make you realize that we are indeed meant to be together, forever.'

I placed the gift on the teapoy. It was a picture of us that I had framed with the help of my father-in-law. His close associate, who owned a photo studio, had made it for me in the morning. It was the same vidhaai picture that had embarrassed me all those years ago—of me weeping copiously in the car when Jasmine was leaving her family behind. Jasmine loved it, and that was the best thing I could have done at that moment to make her realize how much I loved her.

She opened her eyes and saw the frame in front of her. If there was even the slightest trace of frustration left in her heart, it faded the moment she saw the picture. She took it in her hands and kissed the frame.

There was a note pinned to it that she picked up and read.

I am so sorry for the boorish behaviour of late. This picture will keep telling you how much I love you. If I didn't know you, if I didn't have you in my life, I wouldn't be me.

Day and night have become the same to me since the day you left our home. I have come to realize that we can't live separately. I am so gloomy these days because you are no longer waking up next to me. I never meant to demean you, I never meant to hurt you. I never meant to put you through pain. I know an ordinary apology cannot take away the pain I inflicted on you. But please, believe me, you're not the only one suffering.

We hugged each other. Seeing her smile once again, I realized we were soulmates who had drifted apart, and were now drawn together and intertwined by a power far greater than ourselves; two souls intertwined and tangled together. She was a part of me and I, a part of her. In every possible story about my life, she was the happy ending.

* * *

After a few days, when we came back to Mumbai, Karan told me what had happened between Shruti and him. I had no idea about any of these stirring events because Neerav, respecting my reason for undertaking the trip to Delhi, had maintained radio silence. I wasn't really surprised by Shruti's reaction. I heaved a huge sigh of relief when Karan told me that he had backed off immediately and since that day, he hadn't been in touch with Navya; he had even deleted her number after blocking her. However, Karan and Shruti had hardly interacted with each other all these days. Although Karan diligently handled all his responsibilities during the pregnancy period and showed utmost care towards

Shruti, every day was a test of his love as Shruti continued giving him the cold shoulder.

'I had warned you several times . . . don't dig your own grave, but you were on a whole other plane,' I reprimanded Karan when I called him.

Karan said in a distressed voice, 'No . . . I did follow your advice, I did tell Navya that there was, and could be, nothing between us on the very day I told you we were meeting. I didn't do anything.'

'Anyway, let Jasmine and me talk to Shruti, one-on-one when you aren't around,' I said.

I assured him that everything would be fine, although I was wholly at sea about what I should tell Shruti. In fact, I had to first explain the whole sordid tale to Jasmine who knew nothing of any of this.

When I told her, she had an outburst, 'How could he even think of some other girl? Shruti is so supportive, understanding and loves him so much. Ridiculous.'

'Now, let's not go into all that. I've already read him the riot act. What's important is that he never lets his past take control of his present in future. Not even for a minute.'

After I had brought Jasmine up to speed, I asked her to go with me because, more than mine, I knew Shruti would agree with Jasmine's point of view. I had told Neerav to take Karan for a walk when we reached their house. Shruti was very happy to see us after a long time. After exchanging pleasantries with Karan's parents, we took Shruti and went into her bedroom's

balcony. She didn't know why both Jasmine and I had
come to see her in Karan's absence.

'How are you?' Jasmine asked her, making herself
comfortable.

Shruti adjusted the pillow behind her and said, 'How
would I be? You must be aware of everything.'

'Worry is not good for your baby, you know that.'

'I know, but you can't control your emotions, right?
Even if you want to, they tend to overwhelm you.'

When Shruti said those words, I interjected, 'That's
what I wanted to convey to you. Karan didn't let his
emotions overpower him. Although I didn't support his
even meeting his ex-girlfriend, he did. However, he told
Navya that he loves you and only you.'

'How does that matter? He met her secretly and hid
everything from me,' Shruti replied, upset.

Jasmine sat beside her and held her hand. 'So, what
do you expect? Should he have told you before meeting
her? Would that have been okay? Of course not, right?'
Shruti raised mournful eyes to Jasmine, as she continued,
'Why don't you look at it in a positive way? If he hadn't
met her to end it right away, she would've probably
continued to message him and would've tried to lure him
in some other insidious way?'

'He could've blocked her ... simple!' Shruti had a pat
answer. But I gave her another perspective; I wanted to
tell her that Karan really loved her.

'I know he had the option of blocking her; but it
would've always left that soft corner for her in his heart,
right? And now, there's nothing. In fact, he was boasting

that he had made the right decision by marrying you. And trust me, even before you guys got married, we always told him that Navya was never the right girl for him. She was always too self-centred and now, when he is with you, everyone knows how much he loves you. Even you know it. She was never meant to be a part of his life. Even before.'

Shruti was bravely holding back her tears as she asked Jasmine, 'You love each other so much; what would you have done if Aditya had done this to you?'

Jasmine glanced at me and replied, 'Do you think Aditya doesn't have a past? Do you think I don't have a past? Just as Karan did, Aditya also told me everything about his past relationships; and if a ghost from his past had manifested before him, to be honest, I don't know how he would've reacted. Maybe he would've met her too, I'm not sure. There's no point asking him right now because humans react impulsively when such situations arise, and not in a calculated manner. But I would've fully trusted my love for him, I would've had full faith that my love wouldn't collapse like a house of cards. Marriage goes through a lot of challenges, to the extent where you question your own sanity, but in the end, it's all about fighting together against all odds to keep it together.'

Shruti fell silent for a while. Flashbacks of her good times with Karan brought fresh tears to her eyes. Jasmine held her in a firm embrace and instead of consoling her, let Shruti cry out her pent-up emotions. She hadn't been able to share her doubts and her grief with anyone, and that day when she expressed herself to Jasmine, the tsunami of her sorrow poured out without restraint. Jasmine and I comforted her.

After Shruti had gathered herself together somewhat and sat sniffling dolefully, Jasmine said, 'I agree that he should've told you, but he had already told Aditya that he was going to come clean. You discovered it before he could tell you. I, too, agree that meeting her clandestinely wasn't the right thing to do, but you must know by now that your husband is an emotional fool. Not justifying his act here at all, but everyone has a past. And if that suddenly comes back, sometimes you're unsure of how to react. What's important is he didn't dwell on it or let it dominate him.'

I chipped in here, 'He didn't cheat on you. He only thought about you and your child. Remember, the more you suppress your feelings, the more they'll invade your mind. And it has affected you more than you would care to admit. Don't do that. Just get over it.'

Shruti spent the rest of the night curled up in bed, thinking about her whole life with Karan and pondering over our conversation.

Jasmine isn't wrong, Karan loves me, and I love him. Every morning, I try to hate him, but I cannot. Am I stupid? Maybe I am. But after all that has happened, he's fighting to be with me. I'm so consumed by anger that I can't see how much he still loves me. What's worse is that I am trying so hard to tell myself that I'm okay when I'm not.

Shruti had the same dream that she'd had when Karan had been hospitalized. She stood beneath an overcast sky in the pouring rain, screaming because she had lost, hope, control and power. There was no one who could save her from the storm. Not even herself. And therefore, with every sob, she reminisced everything she once had and everything she was about to lose, including Karan. However, today, just as Jasmine had advised her, she attempted to look at things in a positive manner. Maybe her will to scream meant something more, something positive. She still had the strength in her to scream, cry and get upset. And maybe that strength meant that deep down inside, she still had that little flicker of hope; just enough to defeat the undefeated, to rekindle her smile once again and to breathe with triumph in her relationship with Karan.

* * *

The next entire week, Shruti battled her inner demons and Karan could see the hesitation in her behaviour towards him. It wasn't that she didn't care for him. She did. It wasn't that she didn't care for his parents. She did. In fact, she spent more time with his family, who showered her with all the love she sought. It wasn't that she didn't love him, but she had been blindsided by the ingress of Navya into their lives. However, she decided to consciously stay happy and upbeat so that her emotional turmoil didn't affect her child. In any case, the psychological trauma of what she had been through was taking time to heal, accept and move on. She didn't want to take this relationship forward just for the sake of her child—she needed love and respect. A part of her heart wanted to forgive, but a part of her heart wasn't ready to forget.

It was during these times when Karan asked me, 'You've written so many patch-up stories, why don't you give me some ideas that can bring my life back to normal?'

I did give him a few suggestions. He made a video of all their happy moments, that would take her through the happy moments of their marriage journey. He also wrote down his feelings on post-it notes and stuck them around his bedroom walls. His mother had accompanied Shruti for a check-up at the hospital. As he waited for Shruti's return, he wrote the last post-it that mattered the most.

A heap of bad moments has piled up—moments which don't make you as crazy about me as I am about you. At this moment, you may not want to forgive me, but trust me, I'll do everything I can to remind you how worthy our short journey has been. Also, there probably will come a time, somewhere in the future, when I may feel the way you're feeling right now, for whatever reason. Remind me then how you raised my spirits every fucking time I dropped the ball. Remind me how you were a rock-solid support when I wanted to break up with me too.

He stuck the last piece on the wall and closed the bedroom door. He was so excited and eager to see Shruti's reaction when she returned home. He was sure she would love every bit of it and things would magically and instantly revert to normal between them. Now that the stage was all set, and while he waited for her to come back, he decided to quickly catch up on his office emails.

He was shocked to read the latest email. In a matter of seconds, it felt like his life had slipped away.

The termination email left him shaken, enervated and drained. Because of COVID, several employees, including Karan, had been laid off. Being a start-up, the company wasn't able to cope, and a meeting with their financers had resulted in their taking this drastic step. Soon afterwards, he received a call from his chief, saying, 'Karan, we're really sorry but, due to reasons beyond our control, we've been compelled to take this hard decision. However, I wish you all the best for your future. I'm sure you'll do great.'

How the fuck will I do great? They should've at least given me a heads-up. I have a family to support. What am I supposed to do now? My personal life is already fucked, and now I am getting fucked on the professional front as well? What am I supposed to tell Shruti? How will I tell my parents? It seems like I'm trapped in a lifelong battle for survival. First with my life, then my love and now this. I'm afraid I'll lose this battle. Just when I thought my life was back on track, I've been knocked down. Is it because of my one bad decision or was it destined to be so? When will I get back to normal, and how?

He had thought that the road ahead was full of sunshine and rainbows, but now, everything looked hazy. He sat there with welling eyes. Shruti opened the door to their room and saw the room decorated for her. She glanced at the notes on the walls and the fairy lights that Karan had put up for her. The aroma of the scented candles completed the romantic ambience. She read the first note that was right beside her.

The first time I saw you, I knew that the first and the last word of my love story will be your name!

Shruti was flattered and a reluctant smile appeared on her face. She continued reading the notes one after the other, reliving their relationship.

It was like a walking tour through the world of their love story; she glanced at Karan midway to see him teary-eyed. She assumed he was emotional because of the rift between them.

'You just want me to read them, or you want to even say something as well? By the way, this is really . . . wow. I didn't see this coming, for sure. Did you do this all by yourself??' Shruti asked, looking at him, but his head was down. She read another note by the window.

We're adding yet another chapter to our love story—a chapter that'll take me into a new dimension and make me a father. A chapter that I'll be grateful for eternally. The dates are changing so quickly and before we even realize it, we'll be holding our baby in our arms. I'll do more than whatever is needed for you and our child because you both are the purpose of my life. Let's get over the bad days and start planning the name of our baby, the clothes we should buy, decide who changes the diapers and who stays awake all night. We have a lot of things to discuss, rather than dwelling on that stupid phase which I so desperately want to erase from our lives.

Shruti grew emotional and sat beside Karan, who hadn't moved an inch in all this time. She said, 'What happened? You're not reacting at all. I appreciate every note you've written.'

Karan looked at her and broke the bad news without any preamble, 'I lost my job. There were layoffs in the past few days, although I didn't expect to be one of the casualties.'

The moment he revealed it, he dropped his head on her lap and sobbed like a child.

Shruti's blood ran cold as, in that moment, the uncertainty of their future loomed in her mind's eye. However, she remained calm and didn't react impulsively, knowing full well that Karan was already shattered. She put a lid on her sentiments, anger and disappointment and said calmly, 'Don't worry, Karan, everything will be fine.'

Hearing the assurance in her voice, Karan wiped his tears impatiently, 'How? I feel this is God's way of punishing me for my mistake. I wanted to surprise you by doing all this, but fate was waiting around the corner to surprise me with a blunt instrument.'

'You're being too hard on yourself. Just calm down. I am with you.' Shruti held his hand. Her loving gaze gave him the much-needed comfort.

Karan had mixed feelings. 'You're still with me?'

'I was always with you. Even in the worst of times.'

Karan wanted to fade into oblivion as his guilt swallowed him whole, realizing how selflessly Shruti stood by him like a pillar of strength in his life. Not once did she show that she was still hurting by his misconduct or concerned about their future after Karan lost his job. He had broken her heart, but with her every breath, each little shard of her heart seemed to be finding its way back to him.

* * *

It's a strange feeling, being so furious with and hurt by the person who matters most in your life, the one whose soul you thought you knew, but at the same time, having compassion and empathizing with their pain. Shruti wasn't expecting to be so compassionate. The more affection she showed, the guiltier Karan felt. The realization couldn't have been brought home to him more strongly about how his life would've flipped if he had trodden on the wrong path. Every minute, every day, that feeling grew stronger. His parents provided him with their loving moral support; they encouraged him, saying that such challenges and circumstances were inevitable in life's journey, but one had to be tenacious and courageous to overcome these setbacks each and every time. Shruti's unstinting and steadfast loyalty through it all boosted his morale the most. Not only did she become a solid emotional stanchion for him, but that day, she even went a step ahead.

'Karan, I have a few lakhs in savings and you have it too. We can start some business of our own. I know you're looking for job openings continuously, but I can help if you want to start something.'

'Are you serious?' Karan couldn't believe his ears. Even during those days, while she staunchly remained his strength and succour and backed him throughout this bleak period, she remained vulnerable and hadn't completely recovered from the nightmare of the Navya incident. Nevertheless, she cloaked her feelings so that Karan's confidence didn't falter.

She replied that she was indeed serious.

'Oh yeah, there are so many people who are stepping out of their comfort zones and doing whatever they can. Touchwood, our family's financial condition is sound, but I can see you're getting depressed. We can do this for you to become independent and regain your confidence.'

'Your words are more than enough to help me regain my confidence. I don't need anything more.'

If you have your loved ones near you in bad times, when you're at rock bottom, especially that one person who matters the most, it gives you courage; it gives you the strength to stand up, start walking again and resume your journey. Karan wept, realizing how lucky he was to have an angel like Shruti beside him. The mere thought of losing her shook him to the core. He realized how close he had been to committing the deadly sin of adultery, and every day, the very thought of his human frailty made him want to crawl and hide under a rock somewhere. He wasn't proud of the man in the mirror. He hugged Shruti. She hugged him back, but her warmth was still missing.

Karan asked, 'Can't we be together like we used to? Can't we just get over what happened? The enormity of my actions fills me with remorse, and I can't bear to think I've lost your trust in me.'

'I'm with you, and I'll always be with you,' Shruti replied.

Karan coaxed her to sit down by his side and said, 'And I'm really happy with that, my love. But if you can forgive me completely, it'll make me even happier.

The suffering I've caused you and the misery I feel now has showed me the intensity of the devastation in our lives. I would never want to do it again. I know you're with me, but I want us to be like we used to be and try to put this behind us—sharing the little things, watching movies together, going on romantic walks and everything else that we used to do.'

Shruti smiled. 'Karan, I love you and you know my love is beyond measure. But I deserve, at least, the time to gather my soul again. I'll lie in the trenches while we keep sharing our lives with each other until the fear of vulnerability is gone. I'll not promise that I won't get mad at you or have mood swings thinking about those moments. I'll not promise to let it go until I'm ready. But I will stand with you until my heart recovers totally . . .'

Silence enveloped them as they sank into their private thoughts. They looked into each other's eyes, craving love and togetherness. The simple words she uttered after that had a deep hidden meaning and were the reason for the wide grin on Karan's face. He hadn't genuinely smiled like that for what seemed forever.

'I know it will . . . soon.'

That was all she said but those words made him alive once again and sparked the passion he had for her. She had always found a way to read his mind and that day was no different.

'I'll be the one to mend it,' Karan said. The fatigue that he had felt for so long was replaced by an adrenaline rush.

'I know you will . . .' she smiled.

Shruti's hope for herself was putting her broken pieces back together to create a new life where there was room only for love. Love for herself and for Karan. Her hope for Karan was that he would keep that clarity of what true love was, strong enough to combat his demons. Her hope for them was that they would move past this together and live a wholesome life that they and their child deserved, because where there was hope, there was a chance to turn a dark night into a magnificent journey. The ingredients for a happy marriage have always been a cupful of courtesy and kindness, a spoonful of arguments and misunderstanding, a dollop of faith, empathy and love, a pinch of in-laws, and a bit of blindness to each other's faults, slow cooked on a steady flame of devotion. Indeed, marriage goes through a lot of challenges, to the extent where you question your own sanity, but in the end, it's all about fighting together against all the odds to keep it together.

Epilogue

Two years have passed, and the world witnessed transitions in every field since the pandemic; but there was one battlefield with a never-ending loop of problems that even the pandemic couldn't change: marriage. Because abnormal was the new normal here.

Jasmine and I celebrated our fifth anniversary last year, and even now, I keep finding myself in situations where I have to apologize to her every other day for some reason or other. By now, she has mastered the art of spotting the tiniest mistakes I make, and if there aren't any, she manufactures one. After that incident, I didn't promise to never hurt her, but I did promise that I would never do anything that would make her leave me again. We went through some tough periods even later, but we not only lived through them but conquered them, one by one, together. Isn't that the meaning of life, just trying to be a better version of yourself every day? I love each and every aspect of her: the part where she tells me her experiences when out with friends; the part that's goofy all the time; the part that's a child and needs constant reassuring; the part that's mature and handles responsibilities with ease; the part that makes me feel confident. It was only because of her strength that I could overcome the insecurities and anxiety attacks that I had suffered a couple of years ago. My books released after that, putting my mind at ease, and I even started working on some mega projects that opened up new dimensions in my life. I started believing that the pandemic was the great reset that we needed, in order to understand the value of relationships better; to understand human emotions better; to regain a sense of empathy; to get our priorities straight about what mattered and what did not; to enjoy the little happy moments in our life with our loved ones; to stabilize and rethink the course of our lives, and where we were heading; to find joys even in the worst of the worst situations; and to love yourself once again.

In the midst of all this, the way Jasmine has evolved in every aspect of her life makes me fall in love with her over and over again. But one aspect still irritates me, her online orders; and she still has the same standard response: 'I'm telling you, most of these are essential stuff. Who's going to buy them? You?'

And she still prays, 'Please, dear God, don't let my husband be at home when my order arrives.' Neerav still has his bachelor status, at least while I'm writing this. Four years from now, he would have completed as many years in Tata Consultancy Services as a white-collar criminal sentenced to the minimum period of life imprisonment, although we would still have to pay for our own tickets to watch Tata IPL. Loyalty doesn't pay these days, seriously.

He's still looking for the right match for himself after being with us for all these years. By now, he ought to have realized that the perfect match is a myth. However, being Royal Challengers Bangalore fans, we do believe in myths. Perhaps he should start including this on his matrimonial profile, so that no one doubts his loyalty. Even today, whenever Karan and I are in trouble, he's right there, to help us out and to show us what true friends are all about. We don't make best friends, they just happen; and when they do, we need to stick with them because together, the course of life becomes smoother and happier.

Our friendship was like a set of salt and pepper, one such relationship where we not only found profound happiness in each other's company, but we could share anything and everything with each other. And that's the only reason Karan could tell us about Navya, which saved him from making the worst decision ever in his life. And although, to an extent, it was his conscience which didn't allow his crossing of boundaries, I don't mind taking a little credit for bringing his life back on track.

Today, as a father to a beautiful daughter, who takes after Shruti, Karan has far exceeded our expectations of the way he would handle the responsibilities of fatherhood. Their relationship withstood a severe amount of strain, but, hey, you can't have a rainbow without a little rain. With time, Shruti moved on from the Navya debacle and Karan, too, never contacted her.

Eventually, a year ago, Karan got a good job which restored his self-confidence as the breadwinner in his household. Before losing his job, he had invested in cryptocurrencies when COVID-19 had crashed the markets, and the profits he encashed helped him to stay financially afloat until he started working again. Shruti too had resumed her studies, and did everything possible for Karan, their families and her daughter, Sarathi. Shruti preserved all the love notes that Karan had made for her that day. Sometimes, when we were all together, Shruti reminds him of his every mistake and what she had to go through.

We still joke about it and mock him about how miserable his life would've been had he walked away, to which he says, *'I still remember, before getting married, you told me that, within the next couple of weeks, my wedding ceremonies would be over, and my life along with it.* Meri shaadi bhi khatam aur mein bhi khatam. *Now I know, you were spot on, bhai.'*

'Oh, so you mean that your life is finished now that you're stuck with me?'

'No . . . not finished. I meant complete. My life is now complete with you in it. I love you so much.'

They laughed at every mistake they had committed in the past, except marrying each other. That was something they cherished, and together, they made every colour of life look vividly beautiful.